MERRY WISH

By A. C. Salter

This novel is a work of fiction. Names, characters, and events are products of the author's imagination. Any resemblance to actual persons, living or dead is entirely coincidental.

Copyright © 2023 by A. C. Salter

All Rights Reserved
No part of this book may be used or reproduced, in any manner whatsoever without written permission except in the case of brief quotations embodied in critical articles and reviews.

This is a British English version and all spellings are edited as such.

Other books

The Daughter of Chaos series

Eversong
Shadojak
Ethea
Winter's End
Seeking Chaos
Darkest Wish (Prequal)

The Dylap series

Dylap
The Night Fae
Blood Thorn

Merry Wish

Dedication

As always, for my wife, children and grandchildren that make up Clan Salter and give me the inspiration to keep writing. You're more than anything I could want for Christmas.

Merry Wish

1

Frozen Memory

A gust caught the snowflake before it hit the salt water and lifted it above the crest of the next wave. It tumbled between the white spray, escaped the wet and avoided melting into oblivion. The wind carried it over the crashing sea which foamed across the beach, polishing stones and shingles. It danced up the Jurassic cliff, rising on thermals only several degrees above freezing, until it reached the summit, spinning carelessly over the wing of a passing gull, snagged briefly against a tail feather before once again falling free. Falling and tumbling, spinning and glistening, until the gust caught it again as if singling it out from the countless other snowflakes that cascaded along the Dorset coast, leaving the greys and the blues of the sea for the greys and the whites of a small village which was sleeping beneath a thickening blanket of snow. The flake toppled on, meandering through the thatched cottages, the smoking chimneys and the quiet roads, it weaved unhindered through the veil of an old willow tree, over wrought iron gates and across a large drive with a fountain, the wind steering it over the vast grounds to an empty cottage. Black windows stared back at the snowflake, the central one being round with an image of a sleighbell stained upon the glass, staring like an eye as the flake rose over the slate roof towards the huge chimney. Four large pots stood sentinel above the stack, their inky depths hiding untold secrets, teasing the snowflake closer until, like a held breath, the four pots whispered – *bring him home.*

The snowflake ascended once again upon the breath of the cottage, turning endlessly in the air as it travelled inland away from the sea, beating with the purpose it was now given.

****

Alfie Wayfarer stared out of the kitchen window marvelling at the early snow which began to cling to the corners of the sill, gathering as if they were huddling together to watch him. His attention was drawn to a single flake that was caught in an eddy which made it spiral up and down the edge of the glass until it finally reached the opening and floated inside. He smiled as it somehow crossed the room, hovering momentarily before descending to his bare arm, settling upon his skin like it had chosen him specifically.

Wayfarer – come home.

"What?" Alfie murmured as he sat straight, eyes never leaving the snowflake as it finally gave up its frozen body to morph into a single water drop the size of a child's tear.

"I didn't say anything," Alfie's wife said from the table by the phone. She was sitting vigil with a notebook and pen, the call they were expecting would change their lives, and not necessarily for the better.

"I thought I heard something. Probably my imagination. You know how it gets," he chuckled, while transfixed with the glistening bead of water which was now evaporating within the warm room. But not before he thought he caught a glimpse of the sea within the drop. That and what looked like a large cottage.

"I was wondering," he carried on, his mouth blurting out what his mind was thinking before he had the chance to call his words back. "Do you believe that water can hold memories? I'm sure I've heard it or read it somewhere before."

The bridge of Jill's nose scrunched up as she stared at him. Those big blue eyes probably trying to work out if her husband was mad.

"I'm sure I'm right. There is a belief that water can hold memories. I was only wondering if ice could do the same. Well, it stands to reason really. Ice was once water and therefore snow. A single drop could have once been in the deepest parts of the ocean and would have seen endless fish and the terrors of the… I'm doing it again aren't I?"

"Yep," Jill replied, the creases on her nose smoothing out as she smiled. "The Lord only knows what's going on inside your head. I think William's got your imagination."

Alfie checked the time on his watch, William would be home from school any minute. He was hoping the phone call would have happened by then. His son could get as anxious as he did himself. It was only the steel of Jill that kept them together. Especially since the accident.

Planting hands on either side of the chair, he tried to rise and was suddenly struck with a stinging pain in his thigh. He hissed and tried to hide it from his wife, but Jill had seen it. She winced in sympathy.

"It'll pass," he groaned as he rubbed his leg, although there was nothing that could be done when your nerves were misfiring and your brain registering severe pain in random parts of the body adding to the multitude of agony, to the throbbing stiffness in his lower back and the aches in his bones. His body was a wreck, a weak vessel sailing upon an ocean of pain, yet he felt lucky to be alive.

Jill was about to disagree with him when the phone rang. She picked up the receiver and put it to her ear.

"Hello...Yes, he's here but has given his consent for me to speak with you," she said, her jaw clenching as she listened.

Alfie couldn't hear the speaker on the other end of the phone, their solicitor who had been dealing with their case, although the expressions on his wife's face told the story. The furrowing of her brows, the redness that blotched her temples when she was laughing and when she was angry – this was the latter – and the lone tear that was running down her cheek.

"Thank you," she said, tersely, fingers turning white upon the phone. "Your cheque will be in the post."

Despite the barrage of pain, Alfie clambered from the chair, gripped his walking stick and shuffled to the table. Jill's hand felt cold beneath his as he guided the phone back into its cradle.

"It was worth the fight, though. Wasn't it?" he said as he placed a kiss on the top of her head. "We couldn't go down without a fight."

Wiping her eyes she returned the smile, the corner of her lip trembling with trying to hold it together.

"I'll think of something, Jill," he said.

"I don't see how. You can't work, you can't claim any benefits – you can't even answer the bloody phone," she snapped.

"I'll sort it. Something will come up," he said, brushing the back of her hand with his thumb.

"How? The last of our savings will just about cover the solicitor's fees. We've got days left to pay the arrears on the car, the tenancy closes on this place next week and if you haven't noticed, Christmas is less than ten days away. If only that insurance would have paid out we could have at least managed. But for that to have happened…"

'I needed to have died,' he would have finished for her, yet couldn't bare the thought of her agreeing. Instead, he tried not to show the pain as she squeezed his hand to stifle the sob she was holding back. "I got us into this mess and I promise I'll get us out."

Jill laughed through her nose.

"You and your blind optimism," she said, leaning into him.

"You and your open pessimism. We make the perfect couple, balancing each other out," he laughed, then glanced down at his arm and noticed a salty residue where the snowflake had melted. It was in a strange pattern, similar to the Wayfarer's crest of arms – a circle upon a shield with each of the four compass points on it and a sleighbell at its centre. It vanished as he tried to focus on it. It was more likely never there in the first place. Simply a trick of the mind induced by the strong painkillers he was on. The image of the family crest brought to mind his grandfather who he hadn't seen since before the accident. His only surviving relative. Maybe it was time to admit defeat and ask for help.

"We've not seen Bampa in a while. Do you fancy a small drive into town before the snow settles on the roads?" he asked, glancing out of the window again and was relieved to see that the snow had turned to rain. Before Jill answered, the door opened and William came in, dropping his school bag on the floor before heading for the fridge.

"So, how did it go?" William asked, his face a mask of disappointment as he stared at the empty shelves. For a thin boy of thirteen, he could eat as much as Alfie did at mealtimes and snack in between.

"Not as well as expected," Alfie told his son.

William closed the fridge door and sunk into a chair at the table.

"Does this mean no tree?"

"Of course not. We'll get a tree soon and have it decorated. It'll be the best one yet," Alfie said, staring at the boxes of decorations in the corner. He loved Christmas as much as his son and would normally have decorated the house on the first day of December. They had done it like that since before William was born. Starting with decorating the tree. Hanging colourful baubles and trinkets and weaving the fairy lights through the prickly branches. It didn't seem right to put the rest of the decorations up without a tree. And there wasn't much point now that they would be moving out at the end of the following week. He hadn't realised how much he'd been pinning his hopes on the phone call going their way until only a moment ago.

His gaze fell to his hands. Large, thick fingers curling into fists. They were strong, used to hard work and were well adorned with calluses and scratches from his work as a builder. Yet since the accident his skin had become soft. Similar to his body. Once wide-shouldered and strong, now soft and frail. The fall had changed everything – or hitting the frozen ground from two stories up had. Lying paralyzed for hours into the night until somebody found him had been more terrifying than the actual fall.

A spasm suddenly sparked to life in his lower back and he nearly fell to his knees, yet managed a controlled drop into the chair. He reached for the tablets the doctor had proscribed and swallowed two down while Jill handed him a glass of water.

He couldn't bear his wife and son staring at him the way they were doing. He wasn't good at handling sympathy. It was almost as bad as sitting around the house all day with only Molly the mog for company while Jill was out working.

Damn the insurance company and damn the scaffolding company, but most of all he damned himself.

"Let's go see Bampa," he said, trying to distract them.

The ride to the caravan park was done in silence. William was on the back seat playing with his Nintendo while Jill concentrated on the icy road, steering the pick-up truck through the streets of Gloucester. They sold her Mini last month. There was no point in having two vehicles when only one of them could drive. It was a shame that he couldn't sell the truck. It was worth a lot more than her car. His tools bounced around in the back as if asking why they were being abandoned and what had they done wrong? He wondered if he would ever use them again.

Jill drove into Juniper Point, a small site of static caravans for the elderly, and parked outside Bampa's small one-bedroom static. His award-winning roses had been pruned back to nothing and looked in a sorry state in the small soggy garden.

"He's in at least," Alfie said as he caught the curtains twitch in the bay window. Then fiddling with the handle, he managed to open the door before Jill's hand touched his leg.

"I'll get that. The doctor said not to push yourself too hard, remember? One jolt or strain too far and you'll paralyze yourself again. Now do as you're told and wait for me to help you out."

"Yes, Nursey Lamb," he chuckled, although that was for her sake. He hated being mothered. He let go of the handle and waited for her to go around the truck to open the door.

"Now swing your legs out together," she ordered, holding onto his knees and helping him spin in the seat so his back did the minimal of movements, not that it didn't hurt like hell. She handed him his stick and holding his free arm, eased him onto his feet.

"Why do we get so much bad luck?" she asked, staring up at the rain which had decided at that moment to pelt down as if it was at the end of a shift and needed to get through the day's drops before going home.

"Bampa once told me that luck is like an arrow being drawn back on a bow. The more bad luck you draw back, the further the arrow will fly into good luck when it's released."

"If that's the case then our arrow will go into orbit – if it's ever let free."

Together they shuffled up the slope to the front door and were greeted by Bampa who was standing in the doorway with his own cane, and although in his mid-eighties, stood straighter than Alfie did.

"Well, I wasn't expecting you. How are you, my boy? Not too good by the looks of things."

"I've been better," Alfie said as he followed the man who had raised him into the static caravan and hobbled to the sofa.

"And how's little William? Come give your Bampa a hug."

William reluctantly hugged his great-grandfather before hurriedly dropping into a chair and immediately pulled out his Nintendo. Alfie was about to tell him to put it away and to not be so rude when he thought that it might be best for his son to zone out for the conversation they would be having.

"Cup of tea?" Bampa suggested, his smile stretching the worn wrinkles on his face.

"I can make it," Jill said as she crossed into the small galley kitchen. "It'll give you and Alfie a chance to catch up."

"Aye, and a story he must have by the looks of things. So what's happened, my boy?"

Alfie waited until his Bampa had settled into his cosy rocker before telling him. In truth, he hated to talk about the accident. It brought back the terrifying shivers he felt while paralysed. When he thought he would die on the ground, cold and alone.

"In short, I had a bad fall while at work and I'm still recovering," Alfie explained.

Bampa leaned closer, watery eyes roaming over him as they narrowed. Alfie couldn't remember ever seeing him appear so worried.

"You look like you've seen a ghost."

Bampa shook his head, but the fear was still creasing his wrinkles.

"There's something else, isn't there? You're not permanently crippled, are you? You're not…dying?"

Alfie shook his head, chuckling at the term crippled. He must look a sight.

"No. I hope not anyway. I crushed a couple of vertebrae, fractured my pelvis and broke a thigh bone. There's also a bit of nerve damage, but the doctors believe I'll make a full recovery. It'll be slow, but I'm on the mend."

That seemed to please the old man as he relaxed back into his rocker.

"That's is a relief. Yet I sense there is more to the story and why you've turned up. Not that I'm not thrilled that you came."

Alfie took a breath. He hated admitting defeat, admitting failure and loathed to ask for help.

"You're right. There is more to the story," Alfie admitted, setting his stick across his legs as he shuffled into a less painful position. "Because I'm self-employed I'm not entitled to sick pay. I thought the insurance might have covered me but there's a health and safety loophole. I wasn't wearing the right protective gear at the time so the cover was null and void. My own fault, I know," Alfie said, raising his hand as if he could change the fact. And if it hadn't been for the lazy scaffolders who had not bolted the bars in properly, he would never have fallen. Yet he wouldn't go into that. There was no point, and the scaffolders had denied all responsibilities when they were challenged. They probably re-bolted the safety bar in place the moment he was whisked off in an ambulance.

"The truth is, we're broke. The house we're renting is being sold and they want us out at the end of next week and we haven't got a deposit for another home. We're stuck between a rock and a hard place."

Bampa stared at him, grey eyes unreadable as he sucked on his teeth. He closed his lids, his brow furrowing so deep Alfie thought he was in pain. The old man began to mumble something under his breath. It sounded like *it's calling us back*, but it could have easily been something else as those words didn't make sense. Then just as Alfie was about to go to his grandfather, the old man opened his eyes to regard him. They were hard at first but softened as if he was struggling with a decision but relented to the lesser of two evils. Alfie hoped he wasn't going to suggest that they move in with him or that he would cut into his life savings for them.

"You know, the strangest thing happened earlier. Not long before you arrived," Bampa said as he rose to his feet, seeming overly spritely for a man of his age. "We had a small snowstorm. It came and went in a harsh flurry, the wind whipping it up something wild. I was sitting by the window watching it when a single snowflake floated into the room. And I'm flabbergasted from where, as there were no windows open. It landed on my arm and slowly melted. The oddest thing was it seemed to melt into the shape of the family crest. Most probably it was a trick of the mind, yet it sparked a memory of the place I was born and spent my childhood. Samcritsh Bay, ever heard of it?"

Alfie shook his head, his mind wandering back to when he had his own moment with a snowflake. Coincidence? A trick of the mind? Or were they both sharing a lapse of family madness?

"I wouldn't have thought you had. It's a small fishing village on the Dorset coast. Anyway, the family home is still there. Merry Wish Cottage. It's been empty for a while now," he explained as he opened an antique bureau and began to rummage around the drawers and shelves. "I'd totally forgotten about the place. I used to receive rent a long while ago, nothing much – it never stayed occupied for long. And then some holiday agency took it on to let out as a holiday home. That didn't go well either. I tried to sell it of course, but there's a clause which won't allow it. As long as there's a Wayfarer alive, it must be handed down. Of course, with your father dead – God rest his soul - the cottage would go to you. Are, here it is," he said, pulling a shoe box from the back of the bureau and blowing dust from the top. "Now officially I can't give it to you until I've popped my clogs. But that doesn't mean that you can't live in it."

Alfie swallowed the lump in his throat.

"I didn't know you owned a cottage," he muttered, trying to digest the fact that he'd been handed a lifeline. "You've never mentioned it before."

Alfie tried to think back to what he knew of his grandfather's childhood and realised that he didn't know anything. It was something that Bampa never talked about.

"Truth is, I hadn't thought much about it for a long while. Totally forgot, actually. Not until that snowflake landed on me. Anyway," Bampa said, handing Alfie the box. He held it firm for a while, aged fingers going white as if he might change his mind, yet finally released it. "I would like you to move in."

Alfie didn't know what to say. He couldn't decide if what he heard was real or if his grandfather knew what he was saying.

"We can't afford much rent at the moment. Not until I've gotten back to work," began Alfie, but was quieted by his Bampa's hand as he held it up.

"It'll probably need some work, repairs and plenty of maintenance. I've not been down there since before you were born. Like I said, completely forgot about it. I don't want anything from you other than you do the repairs when you feel up to it. After all, it will be yours soon enough."

"Not too soon," Jill said as she came in from the kitchen and set the cups of tea down so she could hug Bampa.

Alfie had forgotten how beautiful her smile was having not seen it in such a long time. Now it seemed to fill the static home.

He returned the smile as he picked up his walking stick and holding it like a bow, mimicked pulling a string back and loosed an imaginary arrow.

"Of course, I'll expect an invitation for Christmas," Bampa said, easing himself back into his chair.

"We wouldn't have it any other way," Jill said.

****

Jack Wayfarer stood at the window of his home looking through the curtains as his grandson Alfie, Jill and little William pulled away in their truck, heading back to Bristol to pack their things up to move to old

Merry Wish Cottage. He swallowed the lump in his throat as they disappeared from view.

"What have I done?" he said out loud, the lie he'd told them feeling bitter in his throat. He had remembered the Cottage, how could he not? He hadn't been there in over fifty years. But it was in his thoughts every day. A continuous longing, a threat that had always been with him and would never leave. A family curse that had claimed his own father when he was no older than William, and although he had no proof, was sure the same curse had taken his son almost thirty years ago. And now the curse had almost taken Alfie. As much as his grandson believed he had been in an accident, Jack knew that it was the curse. Or the snogres that kept the curse alive.

From his pocket he retrieved a large silver sleighbell and held it tight in his hand. It had been in the box he had given Alfie. It belonged at Merry Wish. He had to hold it one last time. He brought it to his face and gazed at the shiny surface, seeing his reflection staring back. The bell had been in the family for generations. As long as Merry Wish had, he guessed. A gift from a saint, or so the legend went. Originally there were four. One for each point on the compass. The one he held was the Northern sleighbell. The other three were long ago lost.

"I had no choice," he said, his breath fogging up the silver surface and distorting his reflection. "Merry Wish has called for a Wayfarer and a Wayfarer must do his duty. If not Alfie, it would be William."

Perhaps together they would break the family curse.

Clearing his throat, he wiped the smudge from the bell and thought he caught the movement of another reflection inside, yet as he tried to focus on it, it disappeared.

Sighing, he set the sleighbell down on the windowsill where it rocked gently before settling, the cross slits on top resting so the N was pointing North.

A bitter wind suddenly rattled the door and he felt an icy draft down the back of his neck. Shivering, he drew the curtain aside and with arthritic fingers, twisted the catch on the window and pushed it open.

He stared at the grey clouds above before closing his eyes.

"It's time for you to return. Look after them, old friend. Keep them safe."

The sleighbell jingled a single sad note. A haunting tone of frost, of ice, of a cold northerly chill. It hung in the air momentarily, echoing around the room before it faded out of the window.

When Jack glanced down at the sill, the sleighbell had vanished. It was as if it hadn't been there at all.

2

Merry Wish

William stared out of the pickup's window at the house they were leaving behind. The small two-bedroom end terrace had been home his entire life – all thirteen and a half years of it.

"Goodbye Charles Avenue," his father said from the passenger seat in front as the pickup pulled onto the main road and his mother drove towards the city and the bypass which would take them to the M5.

"I hear the beach is good down there. World famous in fact," his father said, looking over his shoulder at him, wincing in pain before straightening back up.

William had seen images of the Dorset coast online. They were mainly pebble beaches at the bottom of cliffs. Hard and uninteresting, and he couldn't find any images of the village they were moving to. Samcritsh Bay wasn't easy to find on the internet and when he searched on Google Earth the patch of coast where it was supposed to be was covered in a grey fog as dull and boring as the beaches.

"There'll be fossils too. The Jurassic beasties will be everywhere," his father continued, attempting to cheer him up

It wasn't working.

William glanced down at the two boxes which shared the back seats with him. Molly was in one of them, her green eyes staring out through the bars in the front, meowing her annoyance at the upheaval – William shared her feelings – and in the other box were the dull items which his great-grandfather had given them, along with the key to Merry Wish Cottage; or Wishy Wash, which he decided he was going to call it. He was determined not to like the place he was being forced to move to.

"Have you put the address into the sat-nav?" his mother asked his father, flicking on the indicator as she joined the southbound traffic.

"Kind of. It doesn't recognise the post code or Samcritsh Bay. The sat-nav probably needs an update or something. Anyway, I've put in the rough coordinates of where it should be. We can always ask a local once we're down there."

William sighed as he slouched back into the seat, laying a hand across Molly's carry box and letting his fingers dangle over the bars at the front. Molly batted his thumb with her paw before sulking to the back of the box.

"How long before we get there?" William asked, wondering how far away he would be from his friends. It had been hard saying goodbye to them. At least he could hook up with them again once he got his computer set up at Wishy Wash Cottage. Nothing beats escapism like a joint game of Minecraft.

"About two hours if we don't need to stop. It's not that far," his mother answered, her eyes briefly flicking over him through the rear-view mirror. "We'll be there for lunch and the removal truck should arrive this afternoon. Hopefully tomorrow we can begin putting up the decorations."

"But we haven't got a tree," William argued, stating the obvious. There were only eight days until Christmas and all the good trees would have gone already.

"Bampa said that there are plenty of Christmas trees growing around Merry Wish. You can choose which one you want in the house and your father…" his mother clenched her teeth before continuing, "and I'll cut it down." She shared a look with William's father who was grinning.

"Lumber-Jill," he laughed, which caused his mother to chuckle. "William, have a look in that box. There might be a map in the back of the journal that's in there."

William dragged the box closer and took the lid off. Inside were dusty old papers, a compass and a leatherbound journal with the family crest embossed on the front. He picked up the journal and flicked through it. The yellowed pages were full of hand-scrawled writing, the tiny black letters written so small they were almost indecipherable. He thought they might even be in Latin. And on various pages there were strange diagrams; some of toys, some of a building and others were of various contraptions which William thought could be either inventions or torture devices. There were other pictures. Strange furry creatures that stood upright like a man but had tusks that protruded from their mouths. Whoever drew in the book had a vivid imagination.

"No maps," William said as he flicked through to the back and found large gold writing written beneath the family crest:

Whisper the Key to Unravel and See.

Uninterested, he dropped the journal and picked up the compass. The smooth brass was worn around the edge and scratched in several places across the glass front. It had been used a lot in the past. That was before it spent most of the last century sitting in a box. The face of the compass was made from a fine mother-of-pearl and had intricate symbols set between the quarterly directions. At each of the four compass points was a sleighbell. And midway between each were other symbols. One was of an old drum like the drummer boy would play when old armies went into battle. Another was of a doll, a third a bear and the fourth looked like a tin spinning top. There were others, a child's tricycle, a ball and a hoop, amidst other playthings from a time long ago. A bevel was set around the inner edge with a tiny insignia of the family crest. It could be turned so that the crest could rest over each of the toys in turn.

"Which way's North?" he asked his father as he held the compass flat on his palm and watched the fine needle inside flicker ever so slightly back and forth.

"We're heading South so North would be behind us," his mother answered.

William orientated the compass so that the North pointed back along the road they were travelling from, yet the needle was pointing South.

"I think it's broken," he said before dropping it back into the box and putting the lid on. Well, that was a boring exercise. No doubt the lid wouldn't be lifted again for the best part of another century. He stared out of the window, watching Gloucestershire give way to Somerset and the slate clouds above not caring which county it spilled its rain on. The thick curtains of drizzle fell endlessly, filling the window with all shades of grey.

An hour later they left the motorway and were heading through the Devon countryside, the twisty roads and tight bends making him travel sick, with the sporadic reprieve of being stuck behind slow-moving tractors. It seemed an age before they climbed the crest of a hill and drove past a sign which welcomed them to Dorset.

"Not far now," his father said, winking at him over his shoulder. "We might even pass your new school."

How's that supposed to cheer me up? He thought.

"The holidays start in a couple of days. Is there any point in me going to school before the Christmas break? he asked, saying out loud what he had been thinking since they decided to take him away from his friends to live in a boring village in a boring county in the middle of nowhere.

"Yes," his mother said at the very same time his father shook his head.

"He's got a point," Alfie Wayfarer said, picking the perfect time to go against his wife. One of the rarest of events that ever happened in their family. The only other time he could recall his father saying the opposite to his mother was when they almost bought a dog. But of course his mother had won the argument then, and would also do so now.

"He might have a point, but that boy will be starting school on Monday. It will do him good to meet his new class before the holidays so he knows what to expect when he begins in January," she said, her jaw briefly tightening as she looked across at her husband before staring at the road ahead.

"But he will be a helping hand at home. Especially with you having to travel halfway back to Bristol every day for work."

Way to go Dad. Don't give in, William thought, hoping that his father would stick to his guns.

"I've already spoken to the headmistress. She is expecting him, and he will be going on Monday. End of discussion," his mother said, with the finality of a nail sinking into a coffin lid.

William sat forward, hand rising as if to push his Dad back into the ring, urging him to go another round, but as Alfie Wayfarer nodded to his wife and relaxed back into his seat, William knew his mother had won. He dug his elbow into the ledge below the window and rested his head in his hand, but not before catching his Dad offering him a weak smile. He had tried.

The grey sky became a large black bruise as they descended another hill, his mother steering the truck down a single-track road, a small undescriptive sign indicating that Samcritsh Bay was three miles away.

They didn't pass anyone over the long three miles which seemed more like ten. His mother never venturing above twenty miles an hour should an oncoming vehicle suddenly appear around a bend.

There was another sign, carved in wood and nailed to a gnarly oak by the side of the road. It simply read – Samcritsh Bay. It hadn't won any awards for best bloom, or tidiest village, it wasn't twinned with anything from anywhere and there wasn't even a 'welcome to'. Just the name of the village. That was all they were going to get. No wonder it was hard to find on Google. And from where William was sitting, it was hard to find directly in front of them.

There wasn't much to the village apart from a few stone cottages along either side of the narrow road. The thatch roofing in various stages of rot and the walls in desperate need of painting.

"There's only the one road. Same way in as out so it won't be hard to find Merry Wish," his father said, tapping the sat-nav that had suddenly lost its signal with the satellites. "Look, there's a post office. Pull over and I'll ask them where it is. They are bound to know."

They pulled over to the side of the road. There was no pavement, just the road and then the squat stone building with a thatched roof. His father was going to climb out of the truck when a postman came from the post office and was about to climb onto his bicycle.

"Excuse me," his father shouted as the pick-up came to a stop. "We're looking for Merry Wish Cottage. Can you tell us where it is?"

The postman glared at William's father, nostrils straining as he sniffed, then leaned his bike back against the wall and sidled closer.

"Have I met you before? You look familiar," he said in a thick Dorset accent.

"Err, no. I've never been here before," his father answered, chuckling despite the postman's hawk-like inspection.

"You sure?"

"Yep. I didn't even know Samcritsh Bay existed until a few days ago. Now, have you heard of it?"

"Merry Wish, aye?" the postman said, his scowl never lifting. "Follow the road as far as it goes, then before you get wet turn left."

"Thank you," William's father said, but let his words trail off as the postman had already put his back to them and was on his bicycle and heading into the village proper. He paused briefly to scowl over his shoulder before disappearing around a bend.

"Friendly place," his mother said sarcastically as she put the truck into gear and they began to make their way through the village.

William saw a single shop, no bigger than the post office. It looked like one of those that sold everything but the thing you actually went in for. Beside it was a library which was closed. It gave way to a small stone square with a statue of a man in the middle. His face was turned away from them. On the opposite side was a village hall set behind a cricket green – not that there would be anyone playing for a while. And that was if there were any people apart from the postman.

"It's a fishing village. I expect most of the people are out at sea," his father commented.

"Or at school," his mother added.

Or dead, William might have suggested and wouldn't have been surprised if he had stumbled upon the truth.

The road wound down to the bay itself. It had a shingle beach in the shape of a crescent blocked at both ends by dark cliffs. The waves crashed against the rocks. White spray cascaded in showers with each impact which had carved the cliffs themselves, relentlessly since time began. Much like the people William suspected.

A small track led away from the road. Old oaks empty of leaves lined each side. Their limbs rocked in the wind as they crashed against each other. Broken branches and rotting mulch covered the ground showing that nobody had driven down there in a long time. It was the only way that led to the left, so he guessed that was the way to Wishy Wash.

"This is when the four-wheel drive comes in handy," William's father said with pride as he gripped the differential shift and pushed it forward. "At least we can clear a path for the removal wagon when it arrives.

"Hold tight," William's mother warned as she steered the truck along the track.

The pick-up bounced over or crunched through the vegetation, but they crawled along the track with relative ease. It wound up the cliff, the truck coming extremely close to the edge at times, the tyres catching loose stones which rolled over and fell the long way down to the sea below. William watched them get swallowed up by the dark waves which crashed into the darker rocks and wondered how long he might last if he fell. Not long was his guess.

They crested the cliff and began to wind down into the valley on the other side. A thick fog had rolled in and was covering the bottom of the valley as if a giant cloudy serpent had slivered in from the sea. It wrapped around the truck as they entered the valley, growing thicker the further they descended.

"I can't see a thing," his mother said, putting on the headlights, yet all it did was project two bright cones ahead of them illuminating the fog. Then suddenly a tall iron gate loomed out of nowhere.

Braking harshly, the truck came to a stop inches from the thick bars.

"Is this it?" William asked, unable to see anything beyond the gate.

"Must be," his father said, pulling the catch on his door and swinging it open. Cold air rushed in immediately making everything feel damp. "You coming?"

William's mother nodded as she slipped her jacket on and climbed out.

"Wait for me," William shouted as he zipped his jacket on and joined his parents at the gates.

They were the biggest gates he had ever seen. Stretching the full width of the track and hanging between two large stone pillars. The family crest was carved into one pillar and the name Merry Wish was carved into the other with ornate lettering. Atop both were large stone sleighbells. There was etching around the rim of them but age had worn them smooth.

Beyond the gates was a world of white vapour as if a cloud had dropped from the sky to sit inside the grounds. It swirled to its own wind as if locked in a spectral dance; the main building remaining hidden within its fold.

His father slid the locking bar open, the old metal squealing a complaint but seemed to move with relative ease compared to the age of the gate. Then together they pushed the heavy gates open.

The wind suddenly dropped as if opening the gates released an atmospheric pressure from within the grounds. The white vapour instantly dissolved leaving particles of ice hanging in the air momentarily suspended, frozen in time before floating down to the cobbled ground as snow.

"That was odd," William's father remarked.

"Odd? More like totally absurd," his mother replied. "Must be something to do with the sea air or…" she began but her words trailed off as the three of them took in the scene.

William's mouth fell open as he watched the sparkling powder settle upon the courtyard that lay before them and the large water fountain at its centre. It was similar to the one he had seen before when he had taken a school trip to Barnstaple Castle. There was a square in the town which had a seventeenth-century fountain with a large circular pool which fed from a cylindrical monolith. Although, the fountain before him had a stone figurine of an elf gripping tightly to the central structure, its pointy face set in a rictus grin while pointy ears sat on either side of an even pointier hat.

Beyond the fountain, set in the grounds were statues of animals. William found a large stag, its head raised towards them with huge antlers that glistened with frost. Its unmoving eyes stared at them with judgement. A pair of badgers sat beneath a tall pine, their backs to the trunk while gazing up at the sky.

"This is incredible," he muttered as he took in more of the animals. There were squirrels, deer, hares and what looked like an arctic fox, all carved so intricately that they appeared to be alive.

William might have stared at the animals longer if the sight beyond them didn't demand his attention.

Merry Wish Cottage was much larger than he had expected. Semi-circular steps led up from the courtyard to a huge studded door – the kind that was built to withstand battering rams. The front of the house was set forward from the rest of the main building. It was a home that a rich Lord would have lived in.

A large stained glass window sat above the door. The picture within the red green and gold glass looked to be the family crest. The roof was of a grey slate and the eaves were of a pale wood with an intricate snowflake pattern that interlaced within itself etching the full length of the house.

"How had your Bampa forgotten about this place? It's incredible," William's mother asked, a genuine smile forming dimples on her cheeks which he hadn't seen since before his father's accident.

"I guess we could blame it on age, but if it's always been in our family, then why hadn't he told me when I was younger? I mean, just look at it," his father replied, opening up his arms, stick waving wide to encompass the entire house. "It's magnificent. Shall we?" he asked, holding his elbow for William's mother to wrap her arm around. She nodded enthusiastically.

"Hang on, let me fetch Molly. We can't leave her in the car," William said, rushing back to the truck and lifting the cat box out, Molly meowing in complaint.

"Don't worry Mol, the move might not be as bad as I thought. And bet there'll be loads of places to explore and hunt mice," he reassured the cat. He glanced back at his parents as they wandered arm in arm to the front door. He was about to run to them when something caught his eye.

As he walked past the fountain he was sure he saw the figurine of the elf move, its grin growing slightly wider.

Shaking his head, he pushed that thought away. It must be the trick of the light. Yet as he ran to catch his parents up, he didn't look at the elf in fear of it looking back.

3

Family Discoveries

Alfie hobbled closer to the ancient oak door, trying to balance his weight between his walking stick and his good leg so he didn't need to lean so heavily on his wife. The cobbles beneath his feet added an obstacle as the uneven ground put extra strain on his hips, yet he hid the pain. If Jill thought he was in any discomfort she would insist that he wait in the car. He took in the cottage, his builder's eyes roaming over the old structure in search of damage, or jobs that might need doing. The habit of self-employment - searching out for potential work. Yet the brickwork was solid, the stone free of cracks or damp, the slate roof intact and even the iron guttering was free from rust. It would need further inspection, but at first glance the outside of the building seemed sound.

"It's beautiful. Like something out of a fairy tale."

Alfie rested his hand upon the large brass handle of the door as he searched for the key, the cold metal biting into his soft skin.

"This could be the making of us, you know," he said as he fumbled the key into the lock and turned the heavy mechanism. He expected resistance from the old lock, yet it turned silently and easily as if it were new.

He waited for William to step up beside them before grinning down at both his son and his wife and then pushed open the heavy door.

It swung open with ease, releasing a sudden gust of air that washed over the three of them as if the cottage had been holding its breath and opening the door released it. Then together they stepped inside the large hallway.

It was dark, the only light following them in from outside. Their shadows spread along the stone floor and reached the foot of the wide sweeping staircase. Oak panels lined the walls, matching the dark wood of the furniture and doors.

Alfie found a brass light switch on the wall and turned it on. Old bulbs flickered in the chandelier above before brightening, casting strange shadows around the ceiling.

"That's a relief," Alfie admitted. "I would have thought that the mains would have been switched off and I needed to locate the breaker box. It seems as though we were expected and somebody switched it on for us."

"And cleaned," Jill added as she stepped over to a dresser and ran her finger over the polished wood. "There's not a speck of dust. Did Bampa have a cleaner?"

Alfie shrugged.

"Maybe. Or he may have spoken to the estate agents who have been looking after the property. Either way, let's have a look around."

Molly hissed as William placed her box on the floor and opened the door. She slowly slinked out, sniffed the air, and then darted up the stairs and disappeared down a corridor.

"Molly?" William called as he chased up the stairs after her. He paused before glancing back down. "May I choose my own bedroom?"

"Of course," Alfie chuckled, glad to see that his son was in good spirits. It seemed they all were. Even Merry Wish itself had a feeling of warmth and happiness.

"It's still hard to believe that this is ours," Jill said as she put her arm through his and led him through an open door into a large kitchen with a stone floor. There was a porcelain Belfast sink beneath leaded windows, a large walnut table at its centre and an ancient aga which looked large enough to climb inside.

"You're going to have fun with that," Alfie said, nodding towards the huge oven. No more cramming a turkey into a confined little space."

"I could probably roast an ostrich for Christmas if we needed to," she laughed. "Once I figure out how to work it."

"You'll be fine," Alfie reassured her as they left the kitchen and chose another door to go through. This gave way to a library come study. Two walls were covered in shelves full of books and a comfy chair was sat next to a bay window which looked back out at the snow-covered drive and the fountain. In front of the chair was a writing desk, its polished surface shimmering in the window's reflection.

As Alfie turned to leave the room, a white-hot heat seared down the length of his injured leg. It felt as though someone had rammed a glowing poker through his thigh and calf.

"What is it?" Jill asked as she took his arm.

"Nothing," Alfie hissed through his teeth as he gripped the door frame to take the weight. "I turned too quickly is all. It'll pass."

"Let's find you somewhere to sit down," she said, helping him back across the entrance hall to another door they hadn't tried. It opened into a large sitting room, his walking stick tapping along the stone until they stepped onto a Persian rug. Although it was the first Persian rug he had ever seen with an elaborate snowflake pattern running around its gold threaded edges. It was in keeping with the snowflakes and spruce trees that were intricately carved around the huge fireplace. Along with woodland animals which were carved or etched into the woodwork around the room. There was a field mouse running up a grandfather clock, a badger sewn into the head of a chaise lounge, a leg of which was carved into the shape of a fox. Fern cones and acorns were carved into the oak beams above.

"It's beautiful," Jill said, running her hand across the mantle of the fireplace, her finger tracing the etchings of snowflakes. Inside the hearth was a stack of split logs and kindling ready to light. "The estate agents thought of everything. Shall we light it?" she asked, lifting an antique porcelain lighter the size of her hand. She rolled her thumb over the strike wheel, forcing sparks from the flint block and a single flame caught the oil-soaked wick.

Alfie hadn't realised he was cold until he saw the small flame dancing from the spout of the lighter.

"Why not? There's plenty of seasoned wood in the basket to keep it going.

Jill put the lighter to the finely chopped kindling and the flame caught the curled splinters of wood before greedily rushing across the rest. Within moments the logs had caught and were crackling nicely, heat already filling the room.

Two large Chesterfields sat close to the fireplace, one green and the other red. Alfie lowered himself into the green one to take the weight from his throbbing legs, the old leather feeling softer than it looked.

It seemed strange that such a house existed in his family without him knowing, especially as his family crest was everywhere. It was embroideredd with gold thread into the tall red drapes which hung beside the window, it was woven into a green and gold tapestry which hung above the hearth and was painted on a large porcelain vase which sat upon a side stand.

It was as if one of his forefathers was a wealthy Lord who had abandoned the Cottage, leaving it as it was.

"There's got to be a catch," Jill said as she sat in the Chesterfield beside him, taking his hand. "I mean, yesterday we were stony broke and today we move into a mansion."

Alfie had the same feeling of foreboding. A looming sense that something was about to happen to pull the rug from under their feet. They'd been so unlucky of late that he was expecting another knock. When you've rolled with the punches for so long it was hard to let your guard down, but he couldn't tell Jill that. She liked to be reassured.

"No catch. Unless you count having Bampa here for Christmas. He might enjoy time with us so much that he may want to move in permanently. We couldn't stop him of course. It is his house, even though he seemed to forget all about it."

"That wouldn't be a catch. Your Bampa's a joy and William adores him. Besides, there's plenty of room. The only downside is the distance I must travel to work every day."

"Unless you get a job closer. And I'm sure I'll be able to work again soon. By the state of some of the houses we passed on the way here, there's obviously a lack of builders or even odd job men."

She smiled and leaned into him.

"You'll go back to work only when you're fit and ready and when the doctors give the all clear. I'm not having you going bull at a gate and doing more damage to yourself."

She was going to say more but William chose that moment to burst through the door, his face a mask of horror as he threw himself onto the chaise lounge.

Jill was immediately on her feet.

"What's ever the matter? Have you hurt yourself?"

William folded his arms as he unclenched his teeth.

"There's no Wi-Fi for starts. No phone signal and the plug sockets are so old that I can't plug my Nintendo in to charge. I hate it here."

Alfie swallowed the laugh that almost escaped. It would only serve to make William's mood sink lower.

"There isn't even a TV. This place is the pits," William continued, his gaze drawing towards the fireplace and the warm glow which had been the focus for mankind ever since cavemen had first discovered it.

Jill caught Alfie's eye, the creases of a smile playing at the corner of her lips. They had wanted William to spend less time on screens and this move had done away with them in one fell swoop. She fought hard to control it and not let their son see her so she crossed the room to the window and peered into the rear garden.

"It's only for a short time. We'll get new plug sockets from the hardware store and have an internet engineer come around as soon as possible," Alfie said, hoping that he didn't need to rewire the entire house. You only need to survive for a couple of days."

"And this might keep you occupied for a bit," Jill said from the window as she gestured for him to come. Her smile had turned into a broad grin.

Intrigued, Alfie struggled from the leather chair and using his cane, hobbled to his wife to stare out of the window. What greeted him was amazing.

The rear of the property was a large garden sloping gradually down with the sea as the backdrop. A narrow river wound down the one side where it naturally flowed with the bottom of the valley. Surrounding the valley walls on both sides was a thick woodland of spruce and ferns, their green spiky branches layered with snow and the ground was a blanket of soft pines like something straight from a Scandinavian postcard – maybe Lapland. What made it even more magical was that a cobbled path wound down, joining a small bridge arcing over the river and leading to the sea and a private cove. Waves crashed against the dark stones and further out to sea, just beyond a curtain of fog, lay the edges of a small island.

The entire scene was beautiful, yet it was what lay in the grounds between the house and the river that caught William's eye.

"It's a maze," he said, excitedly.

"Our very own labyrinth," Alfie chuckled as he took in the stone entrance and high walls. A life-size statue of an owl stood sentinel atop one of the walls, gazing back at them with a knowing stare.

"I wonder what's at its centre," Alfie said.

"There's only one way to find out," William answered, gripping the sill. "Can we go, please?"

Both his son's and his wife's faces turned to him and Alfie shrugged.

"You two have fun. I'll make a call to the delivery drivers to explain where they need to go, and then maybe I'll call the estate agents to thank them for making the house so welcoming. That is if that ancient phone in the hallway is still working. It looks like my mobile can't get a signal either."

"You? Make a phone call? How very brave," Jill teased.

"Well I can't very well join you. Not until I've rested a little. You can tell me what you find at the centre of the labyrinth."

He watched them leave, William rushing out ahead of his mother who glanced back from the doorway to blow him a kiss. Alfie pretended to catch it and placed it in his pocket. He was about to blow one back but they were both gone.

Leaning heavily on his cane, he made his way across the living room, making sure he raised his feet high enough so as not to trip over the rug when he heard the jingle of what sounded like a sleighbell. He paused and glanced to where it came from and saw a large silver sleighbell glinting upon the mantle above the hearth.

He stared at it for a moment before shuffling closer. He could have sworn it wasn't there before. He was sure he would have noticed it.

Taking his weight on his good leg he lifted it from the mantle for a closer inspection.

It was old. Like most of the objects in the house. Most probably an antique. There was a large N inscribed on one side and the Wayfarer crest engraved beneath. He gave it a little shake making the exact same jingle as before.

"Where did you come from?" he asked, believing that it must have been on the mantle all along. It was most likely tucked into a corner and a draft had caused it to roll into the centre. He gave it another little shake and smiled at the pleasant sound it created before placing it into his pocket.

He was humming 'Walking in a Winter Wonderland' as he made the rest of the journey to the phone and slumped into the leather chair beside it. The phone was an old rotary from the seventies which required the dialler to place a finger in a numbered hole on the dial and turn it clockwise. He took out his mobile phone, found the number for the delivery company and dialled it out.

After spending a few minutes explaining to the driver's mate how to reach them, he put down the phone and then picked it up again. He retrieved the piece of paper his Bampa had scribbled the estate agent's number on and dialled.

"Hello, Worthington Estate agents and lettings, how may I help you?" said a friendly lady after the third ring.

"Hi, my name's Alfie Wayfarer. My family and I have moved into Merry Wish Cottage, in Samcritsh Bay. I'm calling to thank you for cleaning it and getting it ready for us to move into today. It was most thoughtful."

"Samcritsh Bay? Oh, the strange house at the end of the lane. That used to be on our books a long time ago but we've not had anything to do with that property for years, thankfully. I assumed it was sold ages ago."

"Not sold off, no. It's kind of inherited. Is there another estate agent or letting agency in the area?"

"Not that would cover around here, unless it's one of those online agencies."

"No, I don't think so. Thank you anyway," Alfie said, about to put the phone down but decided to continue the conversation. "Why did you say thankfully, before?"

"Did I?"

"Yes. When you said you had nothing to do with the property anymore. You said thankfully."

"Well, it was a problem property, and not simply because of its location."

Alfie remained quiet, allowing the agent to carry on speaking.

"From what I can remember, nobody ever stayed there for longer than a week."

"Why not?"

There was a nervous chuckle from the other end of the line before the agent began to speak again.

"It seems silly now, but some of the previous tenants complained about strange goings on. Noises in the night, objects being moved or disappearing altogether. I remember one couple who actually tried to get the house exorcised."

"Exorcised?" Alfie repeated. "As in they believed the place to be haunted?"

"Yes. And I must admit, the one time I went to Merry Wish to show clients around, I had a chill down my back as if somebody was watching me. I couldn't wait to leave. That was around ten years ago now. We struck it off our books not long after."

"But it can't have been empty for the last ten years. It feels lived in. And somebody must have cleaned up and put fresh logs and kindling in the fireplace."

"If that is so, it wasn't by us. Maybe somebody from the village," she suggested.

Alfie thought about that. It was possible he supposed.

"Thank you. You've been quite helpful. Sorry for wasting your time," he said and put the phone back in its cradle.

His back beginning to throb, Alfie decided to shuffle to the warmth of the lounge before it became unbearable. And by now he guessed that the fire could do with another log. He took two steps before glancing up at the top of the staircase where he caught movement.

On the top step, standing to attention, was an old toy soldier. It looked early nineteenth century, possibly a cavalier from the Napoleonic wars, its rifle held firm to its shoulder. William must have found it while choosing a room. Why his son had decided to leave it there he couldn't say. Maybe Molly distracted him.

As if the cat was somehow linked to his mind, she appeared, slinking past the toy as she made her way down the steps. But not before pausing beside the lead figure. She gave it a sniff and immediately her hackles went up, her back arched and she hissed.

"It's okay Mol, it's only a toy," Alfie laughed as he watched her dart down the remaining steps and into the lounge.

Shaking his head he hobbled after her, the warmth of the room greeting him as he made his way to the fire. He stooped to pick up a log to place into the hearth, but saw that a fresh piece had already been placed there.

"Jill?" he ventured but by the sound of his voice echoing back he knew he was the only one in the room. And he could hear his wife's laughter from outside, accompanied by William's. Maybe the labyrinth was only small and she had come back while he was on the phone, to keep the fire burning. She was always thinking of things like that.

Smiling, he made his way to the window and peered out. Jill and William were making their way back to the house, faces grinning, their cheeks rosy with the cold air.

"I hope this move works out," he said to the quiet room as he waved out to his wife and son. They saw him through the window and waved back.

"Me too," whispered another voice.

He spun on his heel to face the rest of the room, twisting his lower back and sending a screaming pain up from his sciatic nerve, searing all the way from his spine to his cranium.

Through the agony he saw that he was the only person in the room. Gasping, he gripped the windowsill for support as he attempted to manoeuvre his upper body so his hips were straight. The sleighbell in his pocket jingled with the movement. He hoped it was in sympathy.

He heard the back door open as Jill and William stepped inside the cottage and tried to sit down before they came in. Jill would only worry, especially if he told her about a bodiless voice he heard speak only a moment ago.

"Are, you've managed to put another log on the fire," Jill said as she entered the lounge. "That's what I came back for. How did the phone call go?"

"I didn't stammer once," he said, glancing back to the fireplace and wondering if he had put the log on after all. No, he was sure he hadn't.

"It wasn't them that cleaned the house for us. It might have been somebody from Samcritsh Bay."

"Oh, whoever it was, we must thank them. Did they have anything else to say?"

"No, not really," Alfie lied. Except that they thought Merry Wish was haunted and I'm starting to agree with them, he might have said, but he was a rational man. There will be a rational explanation for the strange occurrences. "How was the maze?" he asked, changing the subject.

"It was easy," William boasted, slumping into a chair. "I could probably do it with my eyes closed. There's only a stone bench at the centre. A bit pointless really."

"Yeah, but how many people can say they've got their own maze at home," Jill said as she removed her coat and dropped it over the back of a Chesterfield. "Not many. Right, I'll try and get hold of the removal men. They should be here soon."

Alfie watched his wife leave the room before turning his attention back to William.

"I see you've found a toy soldier. It looks old, probably an antique. But don't let your mother catch you leaving it on the floor. And definitely not at the top of the steps. You better move it before she sees it."

"What soldier? The only thing I've found in the house is a whole load of boredom."

"You didn't find a little lead figure? It's on the top step. I'm sure it wasn't there when we came in."

William stared back at him with a blank expression.

"There's nothing there, Dad," he said after poking his head out of the door to look. "You're seeing things."

"Probably. It's been a bit of a morning. Perhaps I'll take a quick nap. Can you help your mother? She'll need an extra pair of hands to get things from the truck.

Sulkily, William left the room to find his mother.

Alfie rubbed at his eyes before pulling the sleighbell from his pocket and giving it a little shake. The ball inside jingled around the silver sphere making a tinkling noise, teetering on the edge of giggling.

"Am I losing my mind?" he asked his reflection. The jingling laughter seemed to grow a little louder.

4

A Strange Machine

William hid behind the fountain as the removal truck arrived and watched the men park up and begin to unload. It looked like hard work and he felt a little guilty at not helping, but there was so much around Wishy Wash that he wanted to explore.

He got the eery feeling that somebody was watching him, but everyone was inside the cottage.

A gust of wind picked up a layer of snow from the rim of the fountain and blew it across his face, a faint hint of a tune being whistled carrying on the air.

"Jingle Bells," he said, recognising it.

He swiped an arm across his eyes, and as he did so noticed the statue of the elf staring down at him, its grin seeming to widen.

William was sure it wasn't staring down before. And he was certain that it was facing out of Merry Wish gates.

"Stop looking at me," William snapped, shaking his head and going back to watching the men unload the truck. It was only a statue, nothing more.

Once the men had collected more boxes and began to carry them inside, he decided to run.

He crossed the drive in a half crouch and squatted behind the statue of the deer to take another peek. Nobody was watching, and so he carried on until he reached the wall. He followed it along its length until he arrived at an old wooden door, partially hidden beneath twisted vines.

He thought it might lead to another part of the gardens. Maybe even back to the maze.

The door had a knob in the shape of a sleighbell with the family crest engraved at its centre. He gripped it and twisted, feeling the tumblers inside grate and turn, but mercifully it opened.

He was about to push on the door when he heard 'Jingle Bells' being carried on the wind again. He glanced up to where it came from. Nobody was there. Only the fountain and the statue of the elf.

Then his heart suddenly skipped a beat.

The elf was staring at him again, its head facing in the other direction to where it had been when he was hiding behind the fountain.

"What's going on?" he muttered. Then he noticed something else that was wrong with the scene before him. The deer had vanished. The statue of the huge stag was missing. In its place were paw prints in the snow that lead across the drive and through the trees at the far end.

He might have stayed a little longer to try to work out what had happened, but his mother came out of the cottage, heading for the truck to collect more things and so he pushed on the door and went through before she saw him.

The door scraped over pristine snow, revealing a pretty garden. It was small and surrounded by tall stone walls. It looked like there might have been garden beds making up the borders with a stone badger and an arctic fox playing at its centre.

"They look so realistic," he said and was astonished to see the badger turn its head towards him and the fox leap into the air and dive nose-first into the snow.

William was about to rush back through the door to his mother when he gained control of himself. He was thirteen, not a small boy who was scared of everything.

Taking a breath, he stepped into the garden and slowly trudged through the snow to the badger and the fox, who was still kicking his legs as if trying to burrow further into the drift.

"I won't hurt you," he said, kneeling beside them.

He wasn't sure if badgers were vicious or not, but this one seemed friendly. It sniffed the air before taking a tentative step towards him and then nuzzled against his offered hand. After a moment, the arctic fox stopped wriggling and backed its way out of the hole it tried to create. It cocked its head to the side, long ears flicking snow from the pointy ends.

It was beautiful, its fur as white as the ground around them.

"Hello," William said softly as he slowly stroked him.

The fox's eyes went wide and then softened, its ears lowering as if it had made up its mind that William was no threat.

It then began to bounce and leap on the spot, playfully prancing around William's legs. It glanced at the badger and together they set out across the garden, heading for another door on the far side. They stopped partway to look back at William, an expectant look on their faces.

"Do you want me to follow you?" he asked.

The arctic fox gave a single nod and then proceeded to walk to the door when it stopped placed a paw against it and glanced back at William.

"Why not?"

William trudged across the garden and placed a hand against the door handle, this one was in the shape of the compass, with all the toys intricately carved into the metal work.

Whoever had created it was a clever metal worker.

William looked down at the two animals that were staring back up at him.

"This is so strange. I wouldn't be surprised to find out that I was dreaming," he said as he turned the handle and pushed on the door.

It swung in easily as if the hinges had been oiled.

Inside was dark. Maybe a potting shed or storage room, the light didn't travel much further than a few feet.

He turned back to the badger and fox but they were gone. He would have thought he had imagined them if it wasn't for the prints left in the snow.

Were arctic foxes even native to Britain? He doubted it. They must have been somebody's pets. That was the only logical explanation.

Not letting the thoughts hinder his investigation, he pushed the door open to its fullest and stepped inside.

He caught the grey outline of a window on one wall, the frosted glass covered with snow on the outside and dust on the inside. Using the sleeve of his coat he wiped a patch of dust away and light poured into the room, revealing more of the stone floor and the far wall, which was further away than he had first thought. On the wall was an old light switch.

"I hope this still works," he said as he cautiously crossed to the switch and flicked it up.

A single bulb flickered above, the element inside glowing red before it finally stayed on and filled the room with warm light.

"Wow!" he said, his voice echoing back to him.

The room was easily four or five times the size of the lounge in the cottage and the ceiling was twice as high. And what he hadn't noticed before was that the room was circular, reminding him of the inside of a lighthouse. At the centre of the room was a strange sphere, about the size of a beach ball, although it appeared to be made from black stone.

It was dissected into many sections with toys painted at the centre of each section.

He slowly walked around it, noticing all the toys that were on the compass.

The sphere sat on a small plinth that appeared too thin to take the weight, but it did, and judging by the amount of dust that layered it, had done so for a long time.

The floor was also dissected into sections, with each toy painted in a circle that surrounded the sphere. It was like some crazy attraction at a fairground. Why was it in a room on the edge of a cottage in a quiet Dorset village? It should be in a museum or something.

Further inspection revealed more symbols and a gully in the floor, a shallow trench that ran from the plinth the sphere sat on to a small panel in the wall. It could be a kind of sluice or something. Maybe water ran down the trench and went into the plinth.

"Dad is going to love this," he said to himself and then felt a pang of sadness. Since the accident, his father was a lot less able to get around. And was a lot less enthusiastic about things. But still, he would love to see this.

He ran back outside, across the small garden and made his way inside the cottage. He paused on the threshold and glanced back up the wide drive.

Where the statue of the arctic fox had been only hours before, was an empty space. The statues of the badgers that were sitting beneath the trees were also gone. Had they been real animals all along?

"Very strange," he said, his eyes catching the elf that was perched upon the fountain. "And you can shut up," he muttered, but glanced away and rushed inside should the elf decide to come alive.

He found his father sitting on a stool in the hallway, watching the men unload the truck and begin to unpack everything.

"Dad, you're not going to believe what I've found," he began, but he was interrupted by his mother coming out of the kitchen.

"Where have you been?" she asked, a box of plates under one arm.

"I've found a secret room in the garden around back. Well, it was the badger and the fox that showed me."

"Wait, slow down. Badger and fox?" his mother asked, raising a sceptical eyebrow.

"Yes. An arctic fox. Anyway, they led me to this door and inside…"

"An arctic fox?" his Dad repeated.

"Yes," William snapped, feeling a rising frustration at being interrupted for a second time. "They showed me this door that led to a huge circular room. And inside is this, well contraption, machine, thing."

He realised that what he was saying sounded crazy and so he took a deep breath, calmed his temper and took his mother's hand. "Let me show you."

####

"It's remarkable," William's father said as he leaned against the wall, both hands gripping his cane as he stared at the sphere. "I'm sure I saw a sketch of this in the old journal."

"Remarkable, but what is it?" William's mother asked as she stepped over the pictures on the floor to the large globe at the centre and tapped a knuckle against it. "I mean, is it a machine? And if it is, what is it for?"

"Not to mention the room itself. The ceiling is so high, yet from outside you can't see it," his father said, scratching his head. "It's like the Tardis in Doctor Who."

"Now you're just being silly," his mother said, stepping back to marvel at the object. "Maybe you ought to give Bampa a call. He has to know what it is and what it's supposed to do. But right now, we've got to unpack the rest of the truck. Come on," she said, taking William by the shoulder and guiding him towards the door. "And no sloping off to investigate. There'll be plenty of time for that tomorrow.

5

Lola-Bear

"Molly's gone," came William's voice from the corridor a moment before the bedroom door crashed open. Red-faced and out of breath William all but leapt upon their bed.

"What do you mean, gone?" Jill asked as they both sat up, any hint of a lie-in gone.

William pointed back out of the room, his dressing gown flapping with the motion. "She wasn't there when I woke up so I guessed she was already about the house exploring. I went down to the kitchen to feed her, but she's nowhere to be found."

"She'll be in the house somewhere. There's another door beyond the kitchen we've yet to look in and another into the basement. The Cottage is a lot bigger than our last home. The chances are she's found her way into a room and can't get out."

"Your mother's right. Molly likes the cold no better than I do, so I doubt she'll have gone outside. Let us get dressed and we'll look for her."

Alfie watched the concern on his son's face slowly fade but not vanish completely.

"Okay, but don't be long," he said before ambling back to his own room which was at the other end of the corridor.

"How'd you sleep?" Jill asked him as she rolled over for a hug.

"Soundly. I think I was off the moment my head touched the pillow, you?"

Jill shrugged.

"The same. I could have done with another hour though," she said checking her watch. "It's not even seven yet. And it's Saturday. Although we've got plenty to do. First, let's find Molly. William won't settle until we do."

Alfie reached for the painkillers on the bedside table and swallowed the tablets with water. The small movements he made sent stinging pains down his arms and shoulders. Pain that he knew came from misfiring nerves. Fake pain, as he was told by the experts. Not that it hurt any less. Moving in the previous day had taken its toll on his throbbing body. The worst of it was that he couldn't help with any lifting, which went against everything he was. He was a grafter. Sitting on a chair watching everyone else work put a worse strain on him than any other in the house.

"Coffee?" Jill asked as she slipped into her dressing gown and stepped nimbly into her slippers.

"And a croissant?"

Jill laughed.

"We've got bread so you can have toast. We'll need to drive into Samscritch Bay and check out what the local shop has to offer. I'm guessing that croissants may be a little exotic for the village."

Alfie was smiling through the pain as he shuffled from the bed, grabbed his stick and hobbled after his wife.

By the time he arrived at the top of the staircase, his body was singing an orchestra of pain but what he saw made it vanish quicker than any tablet.

"Molly?"

William's scream echoed around the house, bouncing off the many walls and doorways like a pigeon screech inside a church. His face was turned upwards at the high ceiling and the chandelier that hung from the arched oak beams.

Molly's cage was suspended beneath the chandelier, the handle of the box hooked over the edge of a point, swinging precariously above the hall. Her wide eyes peered out from between the bars with fright. She meowed in complaint, gazing at the floor a long way down.

"How in God's name…" began Alfie as he stared on, calculating the distance between the hall floor and chandelier to be around twenty feet. His builder's mind had already guessed that you'd need a two-level step ladder or tower scaffolding to reach it.

"Dad, we need to get her down. She's scared," William said, his jaw muscles flexing as he clenched his teeth. His eyes brimmed with tears as Jill put her arm around him.

"Who would do this? I mean, how did they even do this? Do you think someone else is in the Cottage? She must have been hung up there at some point in the night."

"I'm sure we would have heard someone," Alfie assured her, although he couldn't be certain. There were rooms in the house that they had yet to investigate. "Perhaps it was one of the removal men playing a prank. A way of getting us back for not tipping them or something," he suggested yet doubted it. There was something extremely strange with the place. Not to mention the machine that Willam had found, or the statues of the animals that were in the garden, now having disappeared.

"I don't care how she got up there. I want her down. She doesn't like it. Dad, do something."

Spurred on by his son's desperation, Alfie glanced about the hall in search of something to use.

"What we need is a long pole with a hook on the end. Maybe we could pull her closer to the stairs and open the cage door. She could probably jump to the landing from there."

"Would a rake do? I think there may be one in the outbuildings somewhere," Jill said as she left them and ran down the stairs and through the kitchen. Alfie heard the back door open and close as she made her way into the back garden.

"Dad, I don't think it was the removal men," William said, his gaze never leaving his beloved cat. "I heard noises in the night. Strange noises around the house."

"It's an old house. They make all kinds of strange noises. Creaking or groaning – that's normal."

"Not those sounds. Well, yes, there were those sounds, but there were also others."

"Like what?"

William stared at him, he bit the inside of his cheek, something he did while thinking over a hard problem.

"Jingling. Like sleighbells, but not quite. Giggling, maybe. Yes. If sleighbells could giggle they would have made the noise that I heard last night. Unless it was in my dream. That was probably it. I was dreaming."

"Probably," Alfie agreed, yet got the feeling that William was right the first time. "But let's not tell your mother. You don't want her worrying."

"Agreed," William replied as the back door opened and closed again, followed by the kitchen door as Jill made her way back up the stairs, a rusty old rake in hand.

Instinctively, Alfie reached for the rake and was immediately rewarded with a searing pain which ran from his fingertips all the way down to his armpit. He tried to mask it but Jill had caught his grimace.

With a tender patience Jill offered him a sad smile before placing her hand atop his.

"I'll do this," she said as she leaned out over the balustrade and hooked a jagged tooth of the rake into the bars of the cage and drew the chandelier towards them. The chains that suspended it creaked and Alfie was worried they may snap. The drop to the floor would bring Molly to an untimely end.

"Careful," Alfie warned as he reached out to steady the chandelier with his stick, holding it while Jill placed the rake down and lifted the cage from off the top, Molly's eyes going wide as she anticipated being let free.

With the cage on the ground, Alfie let the chandelier go where it swung out above the hall before settling into place.

Jill set the cage on the carpet and William opened it, catching Molly as she leapt into his arms, her claws gripping tightly into his dressing gown.

"See, she's safe," Alfie said as William headed for the stairs.

"She's hungry. I'll take her down to the kitchen." But as they began to descend the stairs Molly hissed and sprang from William's grip, her narrowing eyes fixing on a small toy soldier that stood on the top step.

The instant her paws touched the ground she darted along the corridor and into William's room with William chasing after her.

"I don't think it was the removal men," Jill said, glancing up at the chandelier which had settled into its original position looking like it had the previous day and not at all like it had been holding a cat hostage overnight.

"Me neither," agreed Alfie. "But best we don't tell William. You know what his imagination is like. I don't suppose you heard any strange sounds in the night?"

"Sounds? Like what?"

"Sleighbells jingling? Or maybe giggling?"

Jill shook her head.

"I can't say I did. I slept soundly. There's possibly a wind chime in the garden, though. And still many places in the grounds we've yet to explore." She gave him a hug before descending the stairs again. "I'll make us some breakfast.

"Wind chime," Alfie repeated to himself as he hobbled after her, casting a glance down at the toy soldier on the top step. "I'm sure you weren't there when we went to bed. I don't suppose you saw anything while on duty," he asked the lead soldier as he slowly stooped to pick it up.

The Napoleonic five-inch figure stared back, its painted face fixed with a knowing smirk. It had probably belonged to his grandfather and there was likely an entire set somewhere. He slipped the toy into his pocket as he descended the stairs, one step at a time.

By the time he made his way into the kitchen Jill had bread in the toaster and was filling the kettle from the sink. He shuffled to a wooden stool by the window and eased himself down, fixing his face into a smile to hide his discomfort.

"Poor Molly," Jill said as she pulled the toast from the toaster and began buttering it. "She must have spent all night up there. She was put up there by someone. If it wasn't the removal men then it must be somebody from the village. Somebody must have come into the house during the night. The first thing I'm going to do once I'm dressed is go around the entire house and check the locks on the doors."

"And I'll try to unlock the door to the basement. There's probably a key in the box Bampa gave us. While you're up there ask William to bring it down."

"Yep, but you'll be more comfortable in the lounge than perched on that stool. Let me help you through."

Alfie raised a hand. He hated being treated like an invalid, even though that's what he was.

"I'm fine, I can manage."

Placing a piece of toast in his mouth to stop his teeth from clenching, he stood and began to shuffle out of the kitchen, heading for the lounge. He felt Jill's eyes on him as he moved so began to chew the toast, hoping the painkillers would kick in soon. Thankfully she didn't follow him as he couldn't hide the sigh as he sank into the comfy Chesterfield, easing back and smiling as the worn leather creaked.

He felt at home. And not because this was the place he was now living. But felt a true sense of belonging, as if he was always meant to be here. There was a cosiness to the room in the quiet morning. It was almost like sitting in a soft-painted picture of an artist's impression of a Christmas cottage. Snow even filled the corners of the windows, glistening pink in the sun's early rays. It was beautiful, made more so by lazy fat flakes of snow floating down behind it. The rays came into the lounge and caught the many woodland animals carved into the woodwork, almost bringing them to life.

"When did you clean the fireplace out?" Jill asked as she came into the room carrying Bampa's box. She was already dressed and wearing her coat.

Had he fallen asleep without realising it? If he had he hadn't woken with the usual ache down the side of his leg from being in the same position for too long. But then, he did feel at ease and rested.

"I didn't."

Alfie looked at the fireplace and was shocked to find that not only had the ashes been removed and the fireplace swept and cleaned but was already loaded with fresh logs and kindling ready to be lit.

He rubbed his chin as he wondered if it had been done when he first entered the room. It must have.

"Something is happening in the house. First Molly is caged and hung on the chandelier and now this."

She placed the box on the table beside him, the frown never leaving her face.

"I don't think we're in here alone, she repeated for the second time that morning."

"You mean ghosts?" Alfie asked, widening his eyes in mock horror.

Jill playfully slapped his arm.

"No, I don't know. How do you explain what's been happening?"

Alfie shrugged as he took her hand and kissed it.

"There's probably an innocent explanation. Something obvious that we've missed. Maybe the house has a live-in caretaker. Maybe it's somebody from the village. I've felt nothing but a sense of welcome since coming here. And if it is ghosts, I doubt they want to harm us. Maybe it's the Christmas spirit."

"Don't go all Dickensian on me," Jill chuckled as she placed a kiss on his cheek. "Anyway, I'm popping into the village to grab some supplies. I'll ask the shopkeeper if they know of anyone working up here. A village the size of Samscritch and everyone knows everyone's business. I'll take William. I think he needs some fresh air after what happened with Molly."

"I'll sort through this," Alfie replied, tapping the box. "And probably give Bampa a call. If he can forget about Merry Wish I'm sure he could forget about a caretaker."

Jill smiled yet seemed unconvinced.

"I'll see you in a little while," she said before leaving. "Go careful on the roads – it's icy out."

Jill stuck her head back around the door.

"It's me," she said before winking and closing the door behind her.

Alfie chuckled. That had been the line he always used. Well, before the accident at least.

He heard the door slam, the engine on his truck start up and then fade away until he was left in silence.

It was an eery silence. The silence that came on the brink of anticipation as if someone else was in the house listening.

Alfie shook his head before he began believing in ghosts himself.

He slid the box onto his lap and removed the lid. Inside was an array of objects. Keys, paperwork, the journal and the broken compass. He took out the compass and gazed at the strange dial. He'd seen nothing like it before. The N for north was painted over a picture of a sleighbell and had a polar bear beneath it, the East symbol was also a sleighbell and had a narwhal beneath it and the West had a bird in flight, possibly a falcon. The South was slightly different and had a toy drum, the kind that was played as soldiers went into battle. Between these were other objects and toys painted with such detail that Alfie thought the paintbrush must have been finer than a single hair. A bevel around the edge of the compass spun freely and had the family crest engraved into the metal.

He moved the symbol above North.

A jingle whispered from above the fireplace bringing Alfie out of his inspection of the compass. When he glanced up he noticed the silver sleighbell was sat upon the mantel piece. He was sure he had put that in his pocket the previous night.

"Funny, you look just like the sleighbell on the compass. Is it you?" Alfie asked and felt foolish for breaking the silence.

Another jingle.

Alfie looked down at the compass again and found that the red and green striped needle pointed directly at the sleighbell.

Swallowing the dryness that suddenly lined his throat he spoke again.

"This isn't a compass at all but a means of finding things, for finding toys."

Another more excited jingle was the response from the sleighbell on the mantlepiece.

He plucked the lead soldier from his pocket and set it on the table beside the box. He spun the bevel of the compass around until the family crest hovered over a picture of a toy soldier. The needle immediately turned until it pointed directly at the toy on the table.

"Incredible," he said, and then gasped as the wooden soldier changed the position of his rifle and gave him a smart salute.

The actions of the toy startled Alfie and he almost dropped the compass.

He didn't know whether he was dreaming, hallucinating from the tablets he was on or simply going crazy.

The sleighbell jingled again and the soldier nodded curtly towards the mantlepiece before taking a step towards the box. Leaning over so his upper body was above the contents, he used his rifle to point towards the journal – the small carved bayonet making dents in the old leather.

"You wish me to read it?"

The soldier nodded eagerly while the sleighbell jingled excitedly.

Alfie took out the journal and flicked through the pages. It was full of tiny writing, diagrams and pictures. Some he recognised as toys, others were weather patterns and strange devices and some were of the sleighbells. He almost reached the end when the soldier drove his rifle between the pages to stop them from turning.

He'd stopped at a page with large gold lettering, the words read:

Whisper the Key to Unravel and see

"What key?"

The sleighbell jingled and the soldier pointed to the front of the journal where the family crest was embossed into the leather.

At first Alfie didn't know what the toy meant for him to do but as he looked closer he saw that the tiny bayonet was waving over the words that swept around the Wayfarer symbol. The family motto:

Viator Auxilium Quaerentibus Sidus

Alfie had few memories of his father. But one he did have was of him explaining what the family crest meant and more importantly what the words were that were set above the symbol. They were Latin and simply translated as 'Wayfarers help those that seek the star.'

"This is the key, you want me to read it out loud?"

The soldier nodded.

Alfie shrugged. If he was losing his mind, then what harm would reading a simple line out of a book do?

"Viator Auxilium Quaerentibus Sidus," he said, his voice trembling with the strange words as if reading out a spell.

The soldier saluted before stepping back and saluting once again towards the mantle where a young girl now perched upon the carved wood in place of the sleighbell.

She was no older than four or five, wearing a snow-white dress that glistened and sparkled.

Alfie's jaw dropped open.

"Nice to finally meet you Alfie Wayfarer," she said, her voice sounding playful.

She floated down from the mantle, snowflakes trailing behind her in the shape of fluttering wings. She landed gracefully and curtsied, her smile brightening the entire room.

"Are you real?" Alfie asked, stopping short of pinching himself.

"I'm very real, Alfie Wayfarer. As real as you, as real as the snow and as real as Christmas," she replied, leaping into the air and spinning around joyously before landing once again.

"Who, what are you?" Alfie asked, unable to help but smile down at the child. If this was truly a dream or hallucination, then he may as well go along with it.

"I've had many names in many different languages. Some short and some so long that it might take the rest of the day to say in English. Some called me the Great North, the Far North, and for several generations I was known as the White Beast Pola, but I like Lola-Bear."

"Lola-Bear," Alfie repeated. Are you a ghost?"

Lola-Bear giggled.

"No. I'm a fairy. A Christmas fairy."

"And the toy soldier?" Alfie asked nodding towards the small lead figure.

"He's the Colonel."

Alfie thought he should be scared. Scared for his sanity whether this was a hallucination or not, or terrified should what he was seeing before him was actually happening. Yet he neither felt scared nor terrified.

"Toys don't simply come to life."

"You've a lot to learn Alfie Wayfarer and in a short amount of time," Lola-Bear said, her face permanently on the verge of giggling as if she was full to the brim with joy. "The first of toys hold magic. The first ball, the first doll, the first spinning wheel – they are all special the moment a child touches them."

"You mean this soldier was the very first one of his kind to be made?"

Lola-Bear nodded.

"He has been painted many times since he was first created and has had several different weapons. Originally he had only a sword."

"By any chance, did he do anything with my son's cat last night?"

The soldier shook his head and shrugged.

"Colonel?" Lola-Bear pressed before tightening her lips, her fine silver brows going up into her hairline.

The toy's shoulders sagged and he began to nod. He then paced around the table before stooping onto hands and knees, mimicking a cat, his mouth baring teeth."

"She might have attacked you but she's a Wayfarer. You must leave her be."

"It's fine, I think she's learnt her lesson," Alfie said, then addressing Lola-Bear again he asked, "You said I have a lot to learn in such a short time. What did you mean?"

"We're going to do great things, Alfie. There's only a few nights left until he arrives and we've got a lot to prepare before then."

"He?"

"Father Christmas," Lola-Bear finished, twirling around while giggling, making her dress swirl and leaving a small vail of snowflakes in her wake.

"But first we must find my sisters."

"Sisters? There are more Christmas fairies?" Alfie asked as he shuffled to the edge of the Chesterfield, the pain down his leg beginning to rage at being in the same position for too long.

Lola-Bear nodded while holding up three plump fingers.

"Nora-Nu and Flo-Flo. We are the three fairies of Christmas," she said as her bright eyes glanced down at his leg.

"But I see you need some help with that before we go seeking. I'll kiss it better."

Alfie laughed. If only it was that simple.

Lola-Bear brought her hand to her lips and blew him a kiss.

The air around her mouth sparkled, tiny flecks of snow and ice forming into the shape of a small polar bear no bigger than a thumb. It reared on hind legs before silently charging towards him and leapt upon his leg where it dissolved into nothing.

A cold sensation travelled up his thigh, spreading along each muscle and sank down to his bones. It tingled and itched as the cold grew in strength, pulsing up his spine and arcing across his back.

The sensation became intolerable and he gasped before it suddenly dissipated, ebbing away and leaving a floating feeling. His head became heavy and he felt himself sinking back into the chair, eyelids closing until all he could see was Lola-Bear's Silhouette.

6

Samsritch Bay

William stared out of the window as his mother drove the truck down the narrow lane, his head rocked with the uneven ground that brought them precariously close to the edge and the long drop to the dark beach below. Untouched snow lay heavy on the other side, pristine and glistening it covered the trees and hedges and the fields beyond. It was beautiful.

"Can we pick a tree when we get home?" he asked, already having one in mind. While he and his mother were outside the previous day walking around the maze he had spotted the perfect spruce not far from the bridge. It would look great in the lounge.

"I don't see why not. The house is so big we could probably have two or three," his mother replied, her gaze never leaving the road.

They came to the end of the lane and headed into the village proper, the few cottages to either side of the road appearing quiet, the thatched roofs hidden beneath a thick blanket of white. The road took them past the square and the village hall and they found a parking space on a side street beside a small shop that had once been a regular cottage with bay windows but which now had a dull awning that stretched over the front doors.

"Is this the only shop in the village?" William asked, staring around him and the few buildings that made up the heart of Samscritch Bay. There was a small butcher come fishmongers on the other side of the square, a single pub, a bakery and a salon – all of which were made from the usual flint cottages.

"It'll have what we need for now. I can always pick up more from Bristol while I'm at work."

A bell above the door tingled as they entered and again when they closed the door. Inside was as drab as the outside. It was bigger than he thought it would be, with three aisles of food and shelving along the far wall which seemed to contain anything from random garden utensils, stationary and lightbulbs to lipstick and reading glasses. A countertop was at the other end of the shop. Cigarettes and bottles of alcohol sat on shelves behind it, hidden beyond an old-style till.

It seemed the shopkeeper was not present.

His mother picked up a basket and began to walk along the food aisles, picking up a loaf of bread and placing it in.

"You better check the date on that. If it's as old as the rest of the stuff in here we'll be lucky if its best before date is in this decade," William said, laughing to himself until he caught a set of dark eyes staring at him through a mirror which he only then noticed sat on the floor behind the counter. It was angled up, revealing a girl sitting on a stool out of sight. She was around the same age as himself, dressed in faded black jeans and a black hoody. Her scowl deepened the longer he looked at her until another woman walked in from a side door. The magazine the girl had been reading was hastily stowed under the counter before she stood up beside the till, acting as though she had been there all along.

"Catharin, have you seen my…" the woman began before turning to William and his mother. "Oh, good afternoon. Are you shopping for anything in particular?"

"Hi. Just some bread and milk and things. We moved into the village yesterday so need to stock up," his mother replied.

"I thought I hadn't seen you before. I didn't know there were any houses for sale in the village. Anyway, welcome to Samsritch Bay. I'm Penny, the shop owner, and this is my daughter Catharin."

"Thank you. I'm Jill and this is William. We've moved into Merry Wish, the house over the cliff."

"Really?" Penny said, her brows arching up as her lips drew tight. She briefly clenched her teeth before a smile returned. "Merry Wish? I thought that place was derelict. It's been empty for so long that I'd almost forgotten it was there. I expect there's lots of work to do."

"It's not so bad. Somebody has been looking after it."

William noticed that while his mother and the shopkeeper were talking, the girl, Catharin, was glaring at him. Her eyes narrowed through the dark make-up she wore. She was the first person in the village he'd seen that was his age. Maybe the only one. If they were planning on staying at Wishy Wash it might be best to make friends and already he'd made a bad start of it.

He gingerly took a couple of steps closer to her.

"Hi, my name's William," he said by way of introduction, leaving the grown-ups to their own chatter.

"Yes. I heard," she replied flatly, the scowl creeping back and wrinkling the bridge of her nose.

William wasn't good at small talk. Especially with a stranger and doubly so if it were a girl. And it was obvious she wanted nothing to do with him. He was about to join his mother when he noticed a small wolf's head diagram on a black band she wore around her wrist, hidden amongst a lot of other bracelets and bangles. It was the Witcher motif.

"You're a gamer," he said nodding down to the band. "Cool. What machine? I've got a Nintendo but I want a PlayStation," he blurted out faster than he intended.

"P.C," she replied the scowl subtly lifting. "It's old but has a powerful graphics card."

"Do you game online?"

"Of course," she snorted. "Unless I'm here. I've got to help my mum in the shop. Not that we get many customers. Samcritsh Bay is super dull. You?"

"We've got no internet. Most likely it'll be next week before I'm gaming properly."

"Too bad. Could have teamed up on Fortnite."

"You play Fortnite? Cool. Look me up, my tag is Will_Way_terminator492."

Cathrin raised a brow.

"Way?"

"Yeah, as in Wayfarer. It's my second name," William explained. "The terminator part is for fun. I'm not like a real terminator or anything," he laughed, but it sounded fake.

"Wayfarer? As in Samscritch's Wayfarer?"

William shrugged.

"I guess so. Apparently, my relatives came from here."

"You know that statue in the village square is of one of your relatives. Probably a great, great grandfather or something."

William didn't even think to look at the statue. If indeed it was a relative, then why hadn't Bampa said something earlier? But then, he found it hard to believe that the old man could forget that they had a building in the family such as Merry Wish.

"So what's your game tag?" he asked, wanting to keep the conversation on something he knew about.

"Cat_reaper1313."

William grinned.

"I like cats," he said and immediately regretted it. Cat was obviously short for Catherin. What an idiot. He didn't want her to think he was flirting.

Cathrin's cheeks flushed, bringing colour to her pale skin and dark eyes. She met his gaze briefly before glancing down and began to fidget with her fingers. William tried desperately to think of something to get the conversation back on gaming when his mother placed the basket of food on the counter and broke the awkward moment.

Catharin scanned the items through the till and placed them in a bag. When she finished his mother paid, treating them both to a knowing smile.

"Do you go to Lymreg High School?" she asked.

Cathrin nodded.

"She's in year eight," Penny answered as she came over to join them. "She's the only one in the village who goes there so she could meet Willaim at the bus stop on Monday morning. That would be nice, wouldn't it Catharin?"

Cathrin nodded but didn't meet William's gaze. Instead she fidgeted with her bracelets.

"That's good. William will be in the same year. At least he knows somebody now. It might not seem so daunting," his mother said as she picked up the shopping. "A pleasure to meet you both."

"They seem nice," she said to him as they left the shop. The wind had changed direction and now blew in from the sea bringing the smell of salt with the freezing hail.

"I suppose," William offered, pulling his hood over his head to protect his ears from the weather and still wishing he hadn't commented about liking cats.

They were about to make their way across the square to the truck when William paused.

"Catharin mentioned that the statue might be one of our relatives."

"Really?"

They trudged through the gathering snow, making tracks along the crisp white square. The statue's back was to them, the life-size figure was standing erect in a long over coat and a strange kind of tricorn hat which brought to mind pirates from long ago. His mother came around the front of the statue first, and as she gazed up into the face of the figure her eyes went wide. A second later and the shopping fell from her grasp.

"What is it?" Willam asked as he hurried to her side. Then as he looked up into the stony face before him, he realised why.

"It's Dad," he said.

The statue was old, made from a slab of the local rock. It was expertly chiselled in intricate detail. The face bore his father's high cheekbones and strong jaw line. The deep-set eyes and hairline were exactly like his father's, even the serious expression of the brow but with a light mischievous half smile that was typical of his dad, although since the accident William had rarely seen the smile.

The wide shoulders and thick arms were in perfect proportion to his father's, as were the huge hands. One of which was in the pocket of the coat while the other held a sleighbell which bore the family crest.

His gaze followed the statue down the ridiculous pantaloons and stockings to the buckled shoes and the plaque between. Using cold fingers he brushed snow from the old writing and looked closer.

Governor Harold A Wayfarer
Founding Father of Samscritch Bay 1687

Viator Auxilium Quaerentibus Sidus

William tried to read the last line out loud but it sounded strange in his mouth. It was probably Latin or something.

"What was that?" his mother asked stepping closer.

"What was what?"

"I don't know. I thought I saw something sparkle from the sleighbell. Probably just a bit of ice catching the sun."

"What sun? It's thick clouds everywhere." William said, narrowing his gaze on the sleighbell but saw nothing. He was about to re-read the Latin words again when a shadow crept up from behind them to cover half of the statue.

"Magnificent, isn't it?" came a deep male voice.

They both turned and faced a large man with greying hair. He smiled warmly at them as he pulled his coat in tighter. He had a weathered face full of the deepest wrinkles William had ever seen and his cheeks were inflamed as if they had been battered by sea winds all of his life. If he lived here then they probably had. The rubber wellies and yellow southwester hat and raincoat only added to William's assumptions.

"It's a shame that nobody knew the sculpture who carved it. Damn fine work for the time. Even for now. The detail is exquisite."

"Err, hi," his mother said, taking a step closer to William and putting a protective arm over him.

"Oh sorry, how rude of me. My name's Norris-Ogle, Simon Norris-Ogle," he said, holding out a calloused hand towards his mother. "I take it you've recently moved into the village. I thought I hadn't seen you before."

"Yes. I'm Jill and this is William. We've moved into…"

"Merry Wish," the man finished for her. "I know. The village seems to change a little when somebody is in residence. It is the Wayfarer's place. Are you by any chance related to Old Harry?" he asked nodding towards the statue.

"Yep. We're Wayfarers. My husband and William are that is. And I am by marriage."

The old fisherman grinned showing tabaco-stained teeth.

"That's good. There's not been a Wayfarer up at Merry Wish since I was little. Would be nice to go up there and have a look at the old place."

"I'm sure we can invite you up at some point," his mother said, and then added, "Once we've settled in."

"You said the village changes when people move into Merry Wish. What did you mean?" William asked.

Norris-Ogle regarded him for a moment as if only realising he had let something slip, but then he found his smile again.

"Nothing big. And unless you've lived in the bay all your life, you probably wouldn't notice. But you see this stature here of Old Harry. Two days ago he had moss growing in his crevices. A few cracks where water had found its way into the stone and frozen over the winters. Age and weather had mottled the surface but now," he said, rubbing a hand up the smooth arm of the statue. "It looks like it's been polished up new. As if it hadn't been standing in the same place for the last three and a half centuries."

"What?" William asked shocked. "How is that possible."

His mother laughed.

"He's teasing you, William."

"Perhaps," Mr Norris-Ogle said giving William a wink. "But it's good to have the Wayfarers back up at Merry Wish." He tipped his hat as he stepped past them. "Now if you'll excuse me, there's a pint waiting for me in the Broken Compass. Maybe your husband might like to pop into the inn later. Would be nice for the locals to see some of the old Bay blood. And I could possibly organise coming up to the Cottage."

"I'll tell him. Thank you Mr Norris-Ogle."

"Please, call me Simon," he said as he waved them a farewell."

William watched him go, the veil of snow swallowing him up before he passed beyond the square.

"Old Bay blood," William repeated. "Are we really going to invite him up to the house?"

Jill stared in the direction the old man had gone, a puzzled frown dissolving from her face.

"I doubt it. It would be good to meet the locals, though. First, let me take a picture of this statue. Your father will never believe us otherwise."

Using her phone, his mother took a picture of the statue from a dozen different angles, zooming into the plaque between the buckled shoes. Then they climbed into the truck as the snow started to come down hard.

They made their way back to the cottage slowly, the trees along the side of the cliff billowing in as the gales from the sea battered the coastline. The truck rocked from the gusts as it meandered along the dirt track, the wipers going back and forth at full speed but still unable to clear the windscreen long enough for his mother to see properly. Mercifully it wasn't long before the large gates of the cottage came into view and the moment the truck passed beyond them the wind ceased.

It was eerily silent. Snowflakes hung lazily in the air before slowly drifting down to the floor.

"Mum, don't you find that weird?"

The truck came to a gentle stop, the wheels crunching into the snow.

"Weird, yes. But there's probably a natural explanation."

"Like what?"

His mother shrugged.

"I don't know. Perhaps there's a pocket of air up here on the bluff and due to the direction of the wind coming in from the sea and a negative current coming up through the valley, they might cancel each other out."

William slowly nodded, trying to picture two separate winds coming together, but couldn't imagine them cancelling each other out.

"And what about the animal statues that were in the drive when we arrived yesterday. They're all gone."

Jill stared through the windscreen, her eyes narrowing on a deer that was stepping through the trees on the other side of the property.

"I don't know. Maybe they were simply animals that had gotten used to not sharing the place with humans. We showed up and they all went still, trying not to be seen. It's what they do in the wild," his mother explained, although it was clear that she was struggling to believe her own words.

"Come on, let's get inside. I bet your father's been asleep all afternoon."

Lifting the shopping from the back seat of the truck, William glanced up at the fountain and the elf statue that sat atop it. It was looking directly at him. Maybe the head was attached by a swivel joint and could be moved. That must be it. Like his mother said - there was always a natural explanation for things.

He smiled back at the elf and then childishly stuck out his tongue.

He was about to put his back to the stone elf when he stopped, his heart beginning to boom inside his chest.

The elf winked back at him.

William's knees buckled as cold fear shook his core.

"Mum!" he yelled before chasing after her.

He stumbled twice before running through the large front door and slammed it behind him. He dropped the shopping on the floor and hurried into the lounge where he found his father leaning over his mother's phone and looking at the pictures of the statue.

"Remarkable. It definitely looks like me," he said.

William was about to tell them that the elf on the fountain had just winked at him when his father suddenly asked.

"What's that glowing in the statue's hand?"

"Glowing? There was nothing on the statue that was glowing," his mother said as she looked closer at the picture. William joined her, staring down at the screen.

In the statue's hand, the sleighbell was sparkling, so much so that it appeared that the still image was a live video.

"That wasn't there before," his mother said. "How strange."

"Strange," William blurted out, unable to keep it inside anymore. "The elf outside winked at me."

"Don't be silly William," his mother said, in that way which was equal parts annoyed to equal parts humouring him.

His father laid a hand on his shoulder to quiet him.

"I believe you. As it happens, I've had a strange experience myself," he said as he walked across the room to retrieve Bampa's old sleighbell from the mantlepiece.

"Alfie? You're walking without a stick. What's going on?" William's mother asked, going towards his father but stopped as he turned around, cradling the sleighbell as if it was a child.

"I'm fine. More than fine actually. Please, both of you sit down, and let me introduce you to Lola-Bear."

7

The Christmas Mission

"Lola-Bear?" William repeated, from across the room. His mouth fell open as if his jaw was attached by a loose hinge.

Alfie glanced down at the sleighbell in his hand and then back up to his son whose eyes had become large circles as the sleighbell suddenly twinkled brightly, lighting up his face as it morphed into a fairy. She glided to the floor, leaving a trail of glistening snowflakes in the air in the shape of wings before landing and giving a small curtsy.

"How do you do, Jill," Lola-Bear said, her rosy cheeks glowing as she smiled. "And how do you do, William."

"She's a, a…" began Jill.

"Christmas fairy," Alfie answered for her as he put an arm around both his son and his wife and guided them to the Chesterfields, fearing that they might suddenly fall to the floor.

It felt odd to move without feeling pain. He thought it might take him a while to get used to it as agony had been an uncomfortable companion for such a long time.

When they were seated he pulled another chair up so he could sit facing them. There was a lot to explain and no easy way of saying it. As if in sympathy, the Colonel crept from around the box he had been hiding behind and nodded encouragement to him, much to the horror of William and Jill.

"Now there's no need to be afraid. Nothing in this house will harm us," he said, holding his hand out to try to placate them.

"What about outside? What about that elf?" William asked, glancing at the window before studying the toy soldier again.

"Not even the elf. He's a kind of guardian. Nothing in or within the grounds of Merry Wish will harm us. They're here to help."

"Erm, help us with what?" Jill asked as she nervously pulled William away from the toy soldier.

"To save Christmas," Lola-Bear answered.

Jill looked from the fairy to the Colonel and back to him, her lips trembling as she attempted to comprehend what was going on. Alfie couldn't blame her. It must appear as though her understanding of the entire world had been flipped on its head.

"I don't understand. How are we to help save Christmas?" Jill asked, but it was William's sudden question which demanded an answer.

"Father Christmas is real? Really real?" he asked a wide grin threatening to split his face in two.

"Really real. And we've got things to do before he comes. It's a job we Wayfarers have been doing for a long, long time. Well since the very beginning."

"Since the first star," Lola-Bear offered, her joyous smile so infectious that Jill also began to smile.

"The star of Bethlehem?" William asked. "You mean, Jesus, Mary and Joseph and the little donkey and the stable and the three wise kings and all of that?"

"Exactly that."

"I think I need a drink," Jill said. "A strong one."

Alfie shook his head.

"You can't. Bampa is on his way down. He'll need to be picked up from the train station this evening. He's as much to do with this as any of us. Now let me continue. I've a story to tell and I'll try my best to keep it short."

He expected more questions from William and Jill, but mercifully they remained quiet, nervous eyes darting between Lola-Bear and the Colonel.

"The star of Bethlehem was the key to the wise kings finding Jesus. Now as wise as the kings were, they couldn't navigate for fudge, and so they hired a kind of special navigator to guide them. He was a young Hebrew by the name of Elijah. A desert guide who used the stars to navigate – a star navigator, Viator in Latin, or Wayfarer as it had evolved to become. The Wayfarer did indeed guide them to the baby Jesus and well, you know the rest of the nativity. But what you don't know is that once the kings had arrived, the star that guided them dimmed and dropped from the sky. It fell at the Wayfarer's feet. No bigger than a man's fist, it cooled down and as it did, voices whispered to him.

"*The first task is done. We claim you, Wayfarer, to do the next,*" Lola-Bear said in a hushed voice.

Lola-Bear lay a hand upon Alfie's knee and carried on the story.

"Elijah picked up the star and under the direction of the mysterious voices, headed North, travelling to where the North ran out. You see, in the furthest reaches of that land, where the air grows thin, where the night lasts for months and the stars glisten in the cold clear snow, is where magic happens."

"The North Pole? That's where Father Christmas is from," William said.

"Not directly," Alfie said and then nodded for Lola-Bear to explain more.

"For several centuries the Wayfarer built and created things. With the magic around him he was granted long life and good health. Once he finished he was permitted to leave to seek out the man named Nicholas of Bari who lived in Myre."

"Saint Nicholas. The Wayfarer sought out Santa?" Jill asked incredulously, but since she was talking to a fairy, she couldn't disbelieve it.

"Yes. He was to take three sleighbells which were created from the star itself. Each for North, East and West. And from what was left over he created a drum to mark time and which guided the last point of the compass, South. Once he found Nicholas he returned to the North. It was the Father of Christmas's job to spread joy around the world. But the magic of Christmas could only happen with the aid of the sleighbells and the drum. Without them he couldn't reach around the world in such a short time. Although magic is abundant in the far North, it depletes the further you travel from it. And so the Wayfarer agreed to leave and make a new life further South. Not too far that he couldn't feel the pull of the North but far enough to be able to lay guides for Nicholas to follow. Way lines to guide the sleigh and team of reindeer when they travel at star speed."

"Star speed?" Willaim asked. "Is that faster than the speed of light?"

Lola-Bear leapt into the air and spun so fast that she became a blur, her giggling filling the room as sparkling golden dust burst forth before fizzling out of existence. When she came to a stop she was still giggling.

"Star speed is so fast it can go back in time. That's why we need Brother Drum of the South to keep pace. You see, for Nicholas to make his journey every year on the eve of Christmas, he needs to leave in one direction, South. He uses sisters West and East to travel and Brother Drum to keep time fluctuating back and forth. He then needs me, sister North, to guide him home."

"That's how Father Christmas can deliver presents to all the children in the world in only one night," William said.

"Exactly," Alfie said, matching his son's enthusiasm. "And the strange machine that you found outside, you know, the huge sphere with all the toys painted on the floor. That's the machine that creates the anchor. Anyway, I'm getting off track, where was I?

"So the first Wayfarer began his new life here in Samscritch Bay," Alfie carried on, still trying to come to terms with what he was saying. "As far South as he could go where the magic could reach. He kept the sleighbells and the drum safe and every year, on Christmas Eve, he would present the bells and drum to Nicholas, guiding him along the way lines which in turn took him around the world delivering toys to all the children. But as he was no longer in the far North, Elijah began to age. And so to keep the magic of Christmas alive he needed to keep the tradition and the routine going. He settled down and married a local girl. They had a child who they named Harrold Alfred."

"Would that be the Harold A Wayfarer that founded the village and has the statue?" Jill asked.

"The very same," Lola-Bear said with a smile.

"Elijah brought up Harold to help with the tradition of the anchor, which needed to be done every year on

Christmas Eve. The fairies helped of course and the sleighbells and drum, and later the toys. When Harold grew up to have a family he passed on the tradition and so it went through the generations

"To you, Dad," William said. "You're the next Wayfarer."

Alfie nodded.

"But something went wrong. Bampa's Father, my great Grandfather had a run-in with some unsavoury characters. Creatures that would see Christmas finished."

"Snogres," Lola-Bear said, her lips curling back in a fierce snarl.

"Snogres," Alfie repeated. "Snow ogres. They live in the far North, under the veil of magic and want the sleighbells for themselves. They are here and grow stronger the closer that Christmas Eve comes. All we need to do is find the rest of the sleighbells and the drum. Then set them up in the anchor machine for when Santa arrives."

"Two generations of Wayfarers have failed before you, spanning over half a century. If we fail this time, the snogres will claim the magic for their own," Lola-Bear explained, her bottom lip trembling. "The elves will need to leave the North Pole and Christmas will cease to be."

"Why do the snogres hate Christmas so much?" William asked.

"It's the Christmas curse," Lola-Bear explained. "When Elijah first began building in the North, there were two races that existed alongside each other. Elves and snogres. They were not always friendly with each other, so when Elijah asked the elves to help, the snogres immediately saw him as a threat. They tried to curse him, but as they were fighting against a strong magic, the curse backfired and now the snogres are tormented by Christmas."

"How awful. Is there any way to reverse the curse?" William asked.

Lola-Bear nodded and then shrugged.

"All they need do is celebrate Christmas and the curse will be lifted."

"Or sabotage Christmas so it doesn't exist," Alfie added. "And you can guess which it is the snogres are trying to do."

They were silent for a time. Alfie looked to his wife and son who were staring from Lola-Bear to The Colonel, lost in their thoughts as their beliefs had just been expanded. Alfie thought it was a wonder they hadn't run off screaming.

"So, all we have to do is find the sleighbells, toys and drum – put them in the machine for Father Christmas – I can't believe I just said that – on Christmas Eve?" Jill said.

Alfie nodded.

"Although, it's not that simple. You see, we only have one sleighbell. We don't know where the rest of them are. My great-grandfather hid them."

"I might know where there's another," Jill said picking up her phone and placing it on the table. She pointed at the glowing sleighbell in the statue's hand."

"Nora Nu," Lola-Bear laughed excitedly while closing one eye and pointing at the phone.

"Well done. That's two found," Alfie said, feeling that their chances of succeeding had gone up a notch. "Oh, and here's the rub," Alfie added, scratching at the stubble on his chin. "We must not tell anyone. We must act as if we're a normal family. If indeed there are snogres in the village then they will be keeping a close eye on us. And they are more powerful than they appear. Lola-Bear is sure that my accident was caused by snogres wishing to get rid of me so I couldn't return to Merry Wish. She also believes that my parents were killed by them."

It was hard to say. Alfie had never really come to terms with his parent's death. If they were indeed murdered by these foul creatures, then he wouldn't let their deaths go in vain. He was determined to see the mission through.

"Does Bampa know about all this? Is that why he kept this all quiet?" William asked.

Alfie nodded. The first thing he did when he woke up earlier, after he realised that the Christmas fairy wasn't a dream, was to call Bampa. He wanted answers and the old man didn't deny it. He'd explained everything. Including the reason why he kept Merry Wish a secret, believing that he could only ensure Alfie and his family's safety by pretending it didn't exist.

"We've got less than a week to find the rest of Lola-Bear's sisters and Brother Drum," Alfie said as he scratched his chin. He looked down at his son and wife who seemed to be taking it all in well considering the revelations they had discovered. "I'll come with you to the train station, we can pick up Nora-Nu on the way."

"And what about me?" William asked, his eyes darting to the window as if expecting a crazed elf to suddenly appear.

Alfie handed him the compass.

"I need you to stay here and hold the fort. The cottage is stronger when there's a Wayfarer present. Don't worry. Lola-Bear will stay with you, and you never know, you may find the other sleighbell and drum using that compass. We won't be long."

****

"Christmas is real," Jill said as they climbed into the truck. A grin was fixed on her face, her eyes sparkling. "We were talking to a fairy. A Christmas fairy. I should be feeling more surprised, surely. I shouldn't be believing it so easily, but I don't seem to have any difficulty with any of it."

As they drove past the fountain the elf that was sitting atop it gave them a nod.

"Like that," she continued. "That would cause most people to scream."

"Would it?" Alfie asked. He had been thinking the same thing earlier after having a lengthy discussion with Lola-Bear. He thought he ought to be more shocked instead of taking things as they were.

The moment they passed through the gates the storm picked up and was driving snow against the windscreen.

"Will William be okay?" she asked.

"He's stronger than you think. Besides, it'll be a little adventure for him," he answered putting a reassuring hand on her leg. "And Lola-Bear will be there to watch over him. He'll be safer at the cottage than in the village."

"Won't these creatures, these snogres try to get into Merry Wish?"

Alfie shook his head.

"They can't come onto the property without being invited."

Jill shook her head, the grin broadening as she let out a laugh.

"Christmas fairy. And you, healed. You're in no pain at all?"

"Nope. She kissed it better," Alfie laughed, the words sounding as ridiculous as the miracle the fairy performed. "Last week we were broke, on the verge of being homeless and I could barely take a step without groaning from pain. Now look at us."

The storm eased as they descended into the village and the twinkling of stars began to shine through the thinning clouds. Snow covered the ground but Jill drove the truck with ease. Alfie wanted to drive but because it had been such a long time since he was last behind the wheel he guessed he was out of practice. It wasn't worth the risk.

They stopped as close to the deserted square as possible and climbed from the truck. Their feet crunched through the snow as they crossed to the statue.

"You're right. He looks like me. I don't care much for the pantaloons though," Alfie said, gazing up into the face of his elder relative. He read out the plaque at the base of the statue and as the Latin words of the family motto passed his lips the sleighbell in the statue's hand began to glow. Dull at first until it brightened so much it was hard to look at.

"Nora-Nu?" Alfie asked, shielding his eyes from the golden light.

The sleighbell jingled in response, followed by giggling, much like Lola-Bear's.

"We're here to take you back to Merry Wish." As he finished the sentence the sleighbell began to vibrate and fell from the stone hand. Before it touched the ground it began to spin and then rise, flying several loops around his ancestor, then landed before them where it turned into a fairy much like Lola-Bear but a little shorter.

Golden light flowed around her, brightening the wider she smiled.

"Hello Wayfarer," she said while curtsying.

"Nice to meet you, Nora-Nu. My name's Alfie and this is my wife, Jill."

The fairy beamed at both of them, her wings delicately wafting the air as she drew closer.

"I've been hidden for such a long time. Are my sisters close? I have missed them so."

Her smile widened before she laughed, the sound was full of joy.

Alfie was about to answer her question when the pub door swung open and a fisherman paced out. A match burst to life as he put it to a pipe. Luckily his eyes were down and not looking towards them. The pub was at the other end of the square, but still close enough for the fisherman to see them if he was to glance up. Alfie held his breath and willed the man to look the other way, yet it wasn't to be. The fisherman glanced towards them.

His face glowed as he sucked on his pipe, yellow teeth showing through a grin as he waved out.

"Mrs Wayfarer?" he shouted as he began to pace over.

"You know him?" Alfie whispered as Nora-Nu made herself shrink back into a sleighbell and drop into his hand.

Jill stepped closer to him so her words wouldn't be heard by the approaching man.

"We met earlier when William and I were here. Mr Norris-Ogle. Friendly enough – even invited you to the pub to meet the locals."

Alfie met the gaze of the fisherman and put his best smile on. It didn't feel right. He wasn't good with meeting new people.

"Hello Jill, and this must be Mr Wayfarer. How do you do."

"Hi, Mr Norris-Ogle, was it? Please, call me Alfie," he said, shaking the man's hand and wincing at the vice like grip. "Jill brought me down to have a look at my great, great whatever it is, Grandfather."

"Call me Simon," he replied as he eased his grip before looking from the statue and then back to Alfie. "He is the spit of you. You've got some strong genes you Wayfarers. Are you coming back to the pub with me? The local ale is a fine draught."

"Actually, no. Thank you. My grandfather is arriving at the station soon and we're heading over to pick him up."

Simon's eyes suddenly brightened.

"Little Jack? I've not seen him since he left the village."

Alfie glanced at Jill and then back to Simon.

"You know Bampa?"

Simon nodded, grinning with his pipe between his teeth.

"Aye, lad. We used to play together when we were no taller than your knee. We had some fun in the village in those days. Make sure you tell the old goat to come down to the Broken Compass for a catch-up. It would be nice to see him. Unless you want me to come up to Merry Wish. Jill did say I could pop over for a look around at some point."

Alfie felt Nora-Nu shift in his hand, a vibration forcing him to grip her tighter should he drop her. Heat pulsed in his palm and fingers and from the corner of his eye he glimpsed the sleighbell brighten.

"Yeah, I'm sure he would love to catch up sometime," Alfie said as he slipped Nora-Nu inside his pocket. "Oh, is that the time? Come on Jill, we don't want to leave Bampa waiting. Nice to meet you, Simon," he said, giving the fisherman a nod before taking Jill by the arm and guiding her back towards the truck.

"What was all that about?" Jill asked as she closed the door and started the engine.

Alfie brought Nora-Nu out of his pocket and sat her on his lap where she transformed back into the fairy.

"He was there the last time. When it all went wrong," Nora-Nu said, her eyes growing wide and her bottom lip trembling.

"Who, Simon? Was he behind what happened to Bampa's father? The last Wayfarer who lived up at Mery Wish."

Nora-Nu nodded.

"He was there the night Henry vanished. When he was...pushed off the cliffs into the sea," she said.

Tears glistened from the corners of her eyes before running down her round cheeks, the drops changing to form the shape of narwhals. The tiny whales weaved a path down, golden horns guiding their way to her chin before dissolving into nothing.

"What did you say his name was? Norris-Ogle?" Alfie asked, staring into the rear-view mirror and watching the fisherman shrink out of sight. He was sure the man was staring right back at them.

"Yeah. Simon Norris-Ogle," Jill said as her eyebrows went up.

"It sounds an awful lot like..."

"Snogre," they both said together.

8

The Toy Hunt

William couldn't draw his eyes away from the toy soldier that was impatiently marching up and down the table in front of him. He would momentarily come to attention and point his rifle at him and then towards the compass that he was fidgeting with.

"I think the Colonel wishes for you to begin the hunt for the rest of his friends," Lola-Bear said as she approached, her smile seeming to light the entire room. "It was one of your Great-grandfather's favourite traditions."

William couldn't decide which was more surreal; seeing a toy come to life and march before him or talking to a real-life Christmas fairy.

"Toy hunt?" he managed to say.

Lolo-Bear nodded encouragingly.

"Use the compass, it will guide you to the toys that are hidden about the house. Friends that will help us in our Christmas mission. They are quite vital to the tradition. The only toy that has remained free was the Colonel. It was he who has kept Merry Wish clean and ready for your family's return.

The Colonel was eagerly nodding to everything the fairy was saying.

William stared down at the compass, spending time looking at each toy that was painted around the dial.

Trepidation rose within him, mixed with a buzzing excitement; he felt part of the magic.

Concentrating on the compass, he chose the teddy to start with. A toy designed for cuddling. What harm could a teddy possibly be?

Seeing the elf on the fountain wink earlier had unnerved him. And even though he knew now that the elf wouldn't do any harm to him or his family, he still couldn't rid himself of the feeling.

Holding his breath, he spun the bevel round until it lined up with the image of the teddy and immediately the needle turned to face the wall behind them.

"That's good, William. It's a strong signal. Teddy must be close," Lola-Bear said as she floated towards the open door and glided through, a trail of glittery snowflakes floating behind. The Colonel hopped down from the table and ran after her, beckoning for William to follow.

"Okay, I can do this," William said to himself as he rose from the chair and crossed the lounge to the hallway where the fairy and the toy were waiting for him.

Glancing down at the compass he saw that it was pointing towards the cellar door.

"He must be down there," he said and took the few steps to the door and twisted the doorknob. "It's locked."

Lola-Bear landed beside him and pursing her lips, blew a kiss into the lock.

Small snowflakes drifted into the keyhole, glistening under the light from the chandelier and glowing from the darkness within. The strange phenomenon was proceeded by a metallic ping and the rumble of gears being turned.

"Try it now," Lola-Bear suggested.

William gripped the doorknob once again and twisted. This time the door opened, the hinges groaning as the heavy door swung inwards.

"Neat trick," William said as he stepped across the threshold and flicked on the light.

Shallow stone steps led down. They were worn smooth with age and use, spiralling out of sight as they descended.

"Come, William. Nothing in this house will ever harm you. You're a Wayfarer," Lola-Bear reassured him and taking his hand in hers, led him down.

The stairs twisted round three times before coming to the cellar floor which was also made from the same worn stone as the steps. The four walls were flint and seemed possibly hundreds of years old. Boxes and crates were stacked up along two of the walls while a third had shelving which reached almost to the ceiling. But it was the fourth wall which drew his attention. A thick door was set at its centre, a stone arch reaching from floor to ceiling with snowflakes and Christmas trees intricately carved along its edge.

"What's through there?" William asked, checking if the needle on the compass pointed that way. It didn't. Instead, the needle was pointing towards the large stack of boxes on the opposite wall.

"That way leads to the boat house and the river which flows down to the sea. I'm sure no toys are hidden through the door. And I don't think it wise to open it without your father here. The river can be quite treacherous," Lola-Bear warned. "Come, let us find Teddy."

"A boat house? We have a boat house and a boat? That's amazing," William said excitedly. He would ask his Dad to show him when he got back. That is if he isn't too tired. But then, now the fairy had healed his injuries, his father should be as healthy as the day before the accident.

"William, are you feeling ill?" asked Lola-Bear, concern crinkling the bridge of her nose as she looked up at him.

William shook his head.

"I'm fine. Better than fine, I'm still trying to get my head around all this," he whirled his finger around the room to encompass them all. "This magic that is happening to us. It still doesn't feel real. I mean, you've actually met Father Christmas. You know him. And the elves, and the live toys and well, everything. It's remarkable."

"Yes, I can imagine it would be to someone who has only recently become aware. I keep forgetting that. You see, always in the past, Wayfarers - your forefathers – were born into it and were introduced to magic from birth. It was quite normal for them. If you wish to slow down and take things a little bit at a time that would be fine. I don't want to overwhelm…"

"No. I'm good. I'm great. I don't want to slow down, and I don't think we can. Didn't you say we haven't much time?"

"I did," Lola-Bear replied, smiling in a way that brightened up the room.

"Then we better continue this toy hunt," William said while glancing down at the compass. "This way."

He strolled over to the stack of cardboard boxes and began to sweep the compass around until he was sure which of them contained the teddy.

"This one, I think," he said and lifted off the uppermost one, which was the size of a shoe box. He then lowered the second box which was a little bigger.

He brushed the dust from the lid to reveal a quaint picture of a snow-capped forest with a bear dressed in a coat sitting against the trunk of a tree.

William was sure he had found it.

Putting the compass safely in his pocket, William carefully removed the lid to reveal a brown teddy bear dressed in a bright red coat. Its fur was light brown and a little matted and looked old enough to have belonged to a child from the last century or even the one before.

"Hello?" William said, more as a question than a greeting. It still felt odd talking to an inanimate object.

He placed the opened box on the floor and immediately the Colonel marched over and poked the teddy with the point of his bayonet.

"Colonel, that was rude," Lola-Bear scolded, her child's face screwing into a scowl.

The small wooden soldier raised his arms in surrender as he stepped back, seeming regretful of his actions. It looked so comical that William might have laughed if it wasn't for the sudden movement coming from the box which caught his attention.

The teddy began to sit up, its arms rising to grip the side of the box to help pull itself into a sitting position. Once up, his head pivoted on its wide-body to stare with unblinking eyes at William.

"Erm, Hello?" William said.

The teddy's facial expression didn't falter from its fixed position. But then it wouldn't. Its face was made up of two dark brown buttons for eyes and a nose and mouth which had been sewn from black thread.

"Welcome awake, Teddy. Merry Christmas," Lola-Bear said and treated him to a hug.

Teddy hugged her back and then with her help, climbed out of the box and stood on unsteady legs, his gaze falling on William.

William didn't know what to say to the now animated toy. He was about to wish him a Merry Christmas when Teddy made several wobbly steps and hugged William's leg, the top of the bear's head reaching no higher than William's knee.

"This is splendid," Lola-Bear laughed while clapping her hands together. "Now, let's continue the toy hunt. There's plenty more friends to find."

Feeling a pulse of exhilaration sweep through him, William retrieved the compass from his pocket and spun the bevel to the next image of a toy. This one was an old-fashioned spinning top with a plunger that was meant for the child to push down so the toy could gather momentum and keep spinning.

No sooner had he settled the bevel in position than the needle spun about to point directly at the stack of shelves.

He walked closer to the shelves and began to push small boxes and papers aside but found no sign of the spinning top. The other shelves above were similarly cluttered with nothing resembling the size or shape of the toy he was seeking. Although he couldn't see what was on the very top shelf which was easily twice as high as his father.

"I'm going to need to climb," he said while placing the compass back into his pocket.

William had hated heights ever since he fell out of a tree a couple of years ago. His father's accident only added to his fears. Yet this was the time to be brave. His family and newfound friends were counting on him. In a way, all the children in the world were counting on him.

What a responsibility.

Gritting his teeth, William grasped the shelf above him and placing one foot on the shelf on the floor, began to climb.

Slowly at first, should the entire rack begin to teeter and fall away from the wall, William ascended one shelf at a time, but the higher he went the more his confidence grew, his body falling into a rhythm until his hand reached the uppermost shelf and he pulled himself up so he could see over the top.

As he guessed, the top shelf was festooned with dust and old cobwebs, limiting his view but it didn't take him long to find an object the size and shape of a spinning top.

Hooking his elbow around the frame of the shelving, he hoisted his knee up so he could free an arm and reach out to the toy, but as he did so he knocked a grey box and a candle rolled out and over the ledge.

It fell for what seemed like ages before shattering to pieces on the stone floor. He guessed that's what might happen to his leg should he fall awkwardly.

"Be brave," he whispered to himself as he drew his eyes away from the broken candle and Lola-Bear who was staring up at him, looking worried.

He reached out a little further, his hands brushing against the toy and smearing dust to reveal a bright green and red pattern painted on the tin object.

It was the spinning top.

Rising onto the tips of his toes he reached out as far as he could, tapping the spinning top which rocked one way and then the other, drawing towards him as if it wanted to be found.

"Nearly...Yes, I have you," William said as his fingers found the plunger and gripped tightly.

"I have it," he said as he raised it to show the others, yet as he did so his foot slipped from the shelving, and he fell back.

The ceiling rushed away from him as he scrambled to grip the frame, yet all his hands could catch was empty air.

Panic shook through him as he plummeted down, wincing as the ground rushed up to meet him. But it never came.

Opening his eyes he found that he was floating down as slowly as a feather, as if gravity had decided that it didn't want to deal with him at the moment – which was fine with William.

Then he realised that he was being held up by Lola-Bear who had caught him and was gently floating to the ground.

"Thank you," he said as his feet touched the floor, the adrenaline that had been flaring through him making his legs feel like jelly.

The fairy bowed and treated him to a mischievous wink before her gaze fell on the spinning top held in William's arms.

"Welcome awake, Spinney," she said, stroking her small hand down the side of the toy.

William placed the spinning top on the floor by his feet. He expected the toy to come alive as Teddy had done, yet all it did was topple over onto its side and rock back and forth a couple of times before coming to a stop.

"He might need a little help to get going," Lola-Bear suggested.

William nodded and knelt to take hold of the plunger. He stood the toy upright and slowly pushed down.

The top began to turn. A jingling from inside began to tinkle as it picked up speed. Small slits around the upper hemisphere of the spinning top began to whistle the faster it went until William let go of the plunger.

Faster and faster it went, spinning so that the pattern and colours on its surface merged into a blur and the whistling noise took on a piping sound that William thought could be laughter.

Teddy took a step closer to it and reaching out with an arm, rested his paw along the surface of the spinning top, clearing the dust from its body.

"Welcome awake Spinney. Merry Christmas," Lola-Bear said.

The spinning top piped the first four bars of Jingle Bells in response.

"Amazing," William said as he watched the toy spin faster. "Oh, and Merry Christmas. Shall we find the next toy?" William suggested as he retrieved the compass from his pocket and began to wind the bevel. He was eager to see what other toys he could help bring to life.

"We've got a car, a jack-in-the-box, a doll…"

William's words were cut short as Teddy began to jump up and down excitedly.

"You want to find the doll next?" he asked. Teddy nodded enthusiastically.

William set the compass and watched the needle drift towards the large door which led to the boat house.

"Dolly won't be through there," Lola-Bear said. "The needle doesn't discern height, only direction. I'm guessing she'll be above us and down the corridor somewhere."

"Then let us go back upstairs," William said and was about to offer to pick up Spinney, but the toy had already rolled onto its side and began to bounce up the stairs faster than the rest of them, its tune becoming the William Tell Overture.

Stifling a laugh, William followed the fairy and the toys back up to the ground level of Merry Wish.

"It's pointing down there," he said, raising a finger towards the corridor which ran alongside the door to the kitchen.

He walked with his head down, following the needle to the end of the corridor where they came across an old walnut bureau. A brass key was in the lock so grasping it between finger and thumb, William turned it. The bureau unlocked to reveal a desk and pigeonholes of papers and envelopes.

"I don't see her," he said, bringing the compass closer to the desk and moving slowly over the papers. The needle settled on a drawer hidden beneath the lower portion of a shelf. He carefully opened it and found a doll inside.

Delicately he lifted her out.

She was a little smaller than Teddy, maybe six inches high, with dark wool for hair and large blue eyes that had been expertly sewn. She was wearing a tiny red and green gingham dress with a small emblem of a Christmas tree sewn onto the front.

Movement brought his attention to the floor where he watched Teddy jump up and down excitedly with his arms stretched out towards him.

"Here you go," William said as he gently lowered Dolly into Teddy's waiting arms.

As the two toys touched the doll became animated. Her small arms wrapped around the shoulders of Teddy as she drew him in for a tight hug.

"Welcome awake," William said, beating Lola-Bear to the greeting. "And Merry Christmas."

"Merry Christmas Dolly," Lola-Bear repeated as she beamed down at the doll who let go of Teddy and gave a neat curtsy.

"Who shall we find next?" William asked as he raised the compass once more, yet as he was about to turn the bevel the front door to the house opened and his father's voice echoed from the hall.

"William we're home."

Slipping the compass into his pocket, William raced along the corridor and into the hall where he found his mother and father taking their coats off.

"There you are my boy," Bampa said as he hugged William. "And I see you've started the toy hunt. That was always my favourite tradition."

"That's what Lola-Bear said," William replied, hugging Bampa back. "But we've still got plenty to find."

"And we will," his father said stepping into the hall to reveal another Christmas fairy that had been hiding behind his legs. "But first let me introduce you to Nora-Nu."

"Lola-Bear," the Christmas fairy giggled as she flew across the hall to her sister leaving a trail of delicate snowflakes in her wake.

William couldn't help but smile as the two held hands and danced around each other, cheeks flush with joy before coming to a stop and rubbing their noses together.

"Welcome awake," they said in unison and instantly burst into laughter which seemed to be infectious.

Bampa let go of William and took a few steps into the house, his watery grey eyes scanning over the place before settling back on William.

"It's been a long time since I was last here. It hasn't changed a bit," he said turning so he could take one of William's hands and one of his father's. "And I'm sorry for not telling you sooner about Merry Wish. And I'm even more sorry for getting you involved now."

"There's nothing to apologize for," William's father said. "I know why you didn't tell us. You were only trying to keep us safe."

Lola-Bear and Nora-Nu floated across the hall, hand in hand to land in the middle of them.

"Merry Wish wanted you back," Lola-Bear said.

"And Father Christmas needs you, all of you and all of us," Nora-Nu added, waving her arm to include the toys on the floor which had also come closer, the Colonel making a neat salute.

"This Christmas is going to be the best one ever," William said, laughing. "I'll find the rest of the toys."

"And I'll help," Bampa said, squeezing William's shoulder. "I already know some of the hiding places where my father hid the toys. Especially the car. He was always the hardest to find."

9

Flo-Flo

Alfie opened his eyes to find the Colonel standing on his chest, the morning light spilling through the bedroom curtain to light up the toy's silver bayonet.

"Morning Colonel," he said as he sat up, careful not to move too quickly and send the lead soldier spilling across the bed.

The Colonel saluted and then using his rifle pointed to the bedroom door.

"Do you want me to get up and go downstairs?" Alfie asked as he checked the time on his watch.

It was eight. He'd gotten to bed around eleven and found sleep the moment his head hit the pillow.

"Eleven hours. Probably the best night's sleep I've had in a very long time. Okay, Colonel, let's get to the parade," he said and gave a mock salute to the toy who seemed less than impressed.

Throwing his dressing gown on, Alfie made his way downstairs to the kitchen where the smell of bacon was making his belly grumble.

Sitting at the breakfast table were William and Bampa, already enjoying a cooked breakfast while Jill was busy putting sausages under the grill.

"Hungry?" she asked as he slipped an arm around her waist and placed a kiss on her cheek.

"Like a wolf," he replied. "So, what's today's plans?"

Lola-Bear and Nora-Nu flew into the room and each took one of his hands and pulled him to the table.

There were a few new toys that had joined the party since the previous night. An old diecast car was racing around the floor being chased by a jack-in-a-box who was dragging himself along with overly large hands, a goofy grin splitting his clown face. A cricket ball was rolling back and forth between a small wooden ship with a pirate's flag and Teddy who was clumsily trying to catch it, much to Dolly's amusement.

"Today we must finish the toy hunt and find Flo-Flo," Lola-Bear said.

"That won't be that hard. The compass will lead the way. Won't it?" Alfie added as he watched both the smiles on the fairies begin to droop.

"No. It's not as easy as that," Bampa explained. "You see, my father would hide some toys and one or two of the fairies where even the compass can't find them. Just in case the compass fell into the hands of the snogres."

"How do you hide them from the compass? I thought it pointed to where all of them are," Alfie asked as Jill placed a plate of bacon, sausages and eggs before him which made his mouth begin to water. He fought the urge to pile into his breakfast and instead concentrated on the conversation.

"There are two ways to hide things from the compass. One is to hide the toy or fairy within spirits," Bampa explained.

"You mean ghosts?" William asked, his eyebrows disappearing up into his hairline.

Bampa laughed.

"No, my boy. Spirits, as in alcohol. Whisky, brandy, vodka – these will all mask the whereabouts of things from the compass. I remember my father once hid the

Colonel in a crate of wine. He was the last toy I found that year and he wasn't happy about it."

"And the second way?" Alfie asked.

"Running water. A stream or river. There's a small island in the bay at the foot of the cliff which is directly in line with the river that sweeps down our valley. I'm betting my father hid one of the fairies there."

"Then that's where we'll go," Alfie said. "Right after I've finished breakfast."

He dipped a sausage into the egg to break the yolk before placing it into his mouth. He'd been in pain for so long that he had forgotten what it was like to taste good food without the distraction.

"Can I come?" William asked as he rose to fetch his coat.

"I'm sorry my boy. I think it would be best for me to go with your dad, as I've been to the island before. Not to mention the choppiness of the sea this time of year. Besides, Merry Wish will need a Wayfarer present at all times," Bampa said.

Alfie saw the disappointment in his son's face.

"And we need the rest of the toy hunt completing. You could probably get it finished before we return."

"I can help you, William," Lola-Bear offered. "We were a good team yesterday."

"I suppose," William replied begrudgingly.

"And Nora-Nu will go with you to the island. She can help if the tide gets too strong," Lola-Bear said, smiling at her sister. "It's been a while since you've felt the salty brine on you."

Nora-Nu nodded as she flew around the room, nearly knocking the coffee pot over.

"It's been far too long since I swam beneath the waves, to feel the sea, to ride the surf."

Alfie had a sudden thought and the feeling of dread crept over him.

"We do have a boat, don't we?" he asked.

Bampa shrugged.

"I remember a boat. A wooden rowing boat which was tied up in the boat house. Although, with nobody here to keep it maintained it might have fallen into disrepair."

"Or that it needs any repair. If the boat's not sound, you won't be going to the island," Jill said.

"Agreed. Well, not until we can commandeer another vessel," Bampa said as he rose. "Now, let's see if we can get the boat to float."

****

Alfie strode after his grandfather as they made their way along the narrow tunnel which led from the cellar. A cool draft blew from the grey light ahead where the sound of rushing water echoed up. Nora-Nu skipped between them, humming 'The Holly And The Ivy' while gleefully smiling at the way ahead.

"I had no idea this was even here," Alfie admitted as he pulled up the collars of his coat. "You can't see the boat house from the road and Jill didn't stumble across it while walking around the gardens."

"That's because it's hidden from view. You'll see. It's quite remarkable really. Now here we are."

They came to a stop at an arched opening which led into a square chamber. One half of the room was a dock full of clear water which was fed from a canal that led out into the river. Above the dock, suspended with rope, was a wooden row boat covered with a large oilcloth.

"She looks in perfect condition," Bampa said as he pulled the cloth free. "I think we've got the Colonel to thank for that. Turn that winch in the corner and let us put her in the water."

Nora-Nu flew to the corner before Alfie had the chance, and began to wind the winch. The ropes groaned as the boat came down, but it worked mercifully well for its age.

"I'm impressed. It's been up there for the best part of eighty years and hasn't seized. There's not even a spec of rust and being this close to the sea it should have been coated in the stuff," Alfie said as he grasped a pair of oars from a bracket on the wall.

"Indeed. Like the rest of Merry Wish, the cottage seems to take good care of herself and the things within her grounds."

Alfie held the boat steady as Bampa gingerly climbed in. The boat dipped in the water, rocking gently against the dock wall. He then unwound the lashing and climbed in himself, placing the oars into the pivot points and began to row. A smile curled his lips as he felt all the muscles in his body working without a hint of pain.

"Have you rowed a boat before?" Bampa asked as he rested against the gunnel.

Alfie shook his head.

"How hard can it be?" he asked and wondered if those words alone would doom him to sink, simply to make a point.

He pulled two more strokes and felt the current pull the boat out into the river proper, drawing them away from the boat house and out into the fast water, picking up speed swifter than he would have liked.

"Are you sure you can handle her, my boy?"

The boat rose and fell as it turned into the current and began to flow down the valley with the fast-flowing water.

"Yeah, no problem," Alfie said as he lowered the oars into the water in an attempt to slow the vessel but it was no good, they instead went faster.

Nora-Nu stood on the bow with her arms and wings spread out to catch the wind, laughing with joy. And seemingly oblivious to the disaster that may befall them should they hit a rock.

Ahead of them, rolling waves from the sea crashed against the river water, throwing white spray and foam into the air.

"Brace yourselves," Alfie warned as he gave up trying to control the boat, pulled the oars in and gripped tightly to the gunnel.

The hull hit the sea hard, rocked up and over the first wave and cascaded down the other side. Alfie was almost flung from the boat but it seemed that Bampa and Nora-Nu were enjoying the thrill of the ride.

Again they hit another wave, rocking them up and down and the vessel began to turn side on to the watery onslaught.

"I think it's time to swim," Bampa said, treating Nora-Nu to a wink. "Just like when I was a child."

Nora-Nu smiled back at him before leaping into the air and diving into the next wave.

"Swim?" Alfie shouted as he rushed to where the fairy had disappeared beneath the gurgling surface, but his worry evaporated as he watched Nora-Nu transform into a beautiful narwhal.

A long golden horn shot out of the water followed by the rest of the amazing creature, truly seeming like the unicorn of the sea.

"Quickly, make a loop at the end of the rope and toss it overboard," Bampa ordered.

Alfie did as he was told, making a slip-knot loop and throwing it over.

Nora-Nu turned in the water and drove her horn through the loop in the rope before turning back against the waves.

Alfie fell back into his seat as the boat righted itself and was propelled over the next wave, the hull cutting through the water with ease.

"Amazing," Alfie said as a laugh escaped him. "Nora-Nu is a narwhal."

"Yes, my boy. She is of the sea like Lola-Bear is of the land. She has the power to turn into a ferocious polar bear. It's quite scary."

"And Flo-Flo?"

Bampa stared ahead, towards the island they were fast approaching.

"She is of the air so is a bird. A peregrine falcon if I'm not mistaken. And just as joyful as her sisters, although…"

Bampa began to chuckle, his mind seemingly travelling to a faraway memory.

"Although what?" Alfie asked as the boat slowed and the hull scraped against the shingle beach of the island.

"You will see."

Alfie would have pressed his grandfather more about what he meant about that last comment if it wasn't for the fact that the boat was slipping back into the water.

He leapt out and grasping the rope, pulled the boat a few feet free of the waves with the help of Nora-Nu who had returned to her childlike form.

"That's far enough, she'll be safe here," Bampa said as he made himself comfortable in the boat. "I'll see you soon. The island isn't that big so it won't take you long to find her."

Alfie surveyed the beach that led up into a corps of windswept trees. Beyond the tree line was a small hillock covered in wild gorse which might have been a pretty yellow or purple colour in the warmer months but was bare in winter. Beyond that were a few black rocks which bore the brunt of the sea as waves crashed against them. The beach on that side was also shingle. He could hear the water dragging the larger rocks back and forth, grinding them into pebbles and sand.

"It's so lonely here," Nora-Nu said as she took his hand and began to lead him away from the beach. "Poor Flo-Flo. She isn't going to be happy being left here alone for so long. Come, we'd better find her."

Alfie removed the compass from his pocket which had already been set to find Flo-Flo.

"It's working," he said as he watched the needle point in the direction more central to the island. "I think she's in one of those trees," he said, striding towards the small corps of ferns.

He leaned into the wind and tried his best to shelter the compass from the spray which swept sideways across the island.

"She is near – I can feel my sister," Nora-Nu said as she spread her wings and flew closer to the branches of the closest fern.

Alfie kept pace with her, searching the lower branches and around the ground, but with decades since the fairy had been hidden, the island could have changed so much. Trees may have fallen, new plants grown, and even rocks may have slipped.

He followed the needle which led him directly to a tall spruce, its trunk made crooked over the years of persistent wind.

"She's around here somewhere…Ha. I think I've found her," Alfie said as he brushed a patch of moss aside to reveal a small hollow. He reached his hand inside and retrieved a small silver orb. It was a sleighbell.

Bringing it closer to his lips so his words wouldn't be drawn away by the weather he said the family motto.

Instantly, the sleighbell began to sparkle before bursting into a ball of snowflakes which coalesced in circles. A figure formed first into a bird and then into a small girl the same age as Nora-Nu.

"Hi there little one," Alfie said as he held out a hand to her.

The small fairy folded her arms and glared back at him, chin raised and her lips becoming tight with defiance.

"My name is Flo-Flo," she said, the air around her sparkling with nervous energy. "Where is the Wayfarer?"

Alfie leaned away from the fairy to give her space. She seemed ready to thump him in the mouth.

"I am the Wayfarer," he explained. Jack is my grandfather."

"Jack is but a boy," Flo-Flo replied, her frown growing incredibly deeper. "Something isn't right. Where are my sisters?"

"I'm here Flo-Flo," Nora-Nu shouted joyously as she swooped down to embrace Flo-Flo.

The pair of fairies spun around, holding hands before laughing together. They finished with rubbing each other's noses.

"Flo-Flo, it's been a long time since we were last awoken. This man is indeed the grandson of Jack. Come, we must return to Merry Wish. We've more toys to waken and Lola-Bear will be desperate to see you. And Jack is waiting back at the boat."

"And hopefully the row back won't be as choppy as the way here. The wind is beginning to pick up," Alfie said, a sudden gust buffeting into him and almost bowling him over.

"Oh, it won't be," Nor-Nu said with confidence as she skipped ahead holding hands with Flo-Flo. "My sister will ask the wind nicely if it'll calm."

Ask the wind nicely? Alfie thought.

Jack rose to his feet as he noticed their approach, the boat rocking and unbalancing him, but he managed to wedge his walking stick tight into the gunnel for support.

"Flo-Flo," Bampa said as both fairies embraced him. "Merry Christmas."

"Merry Christmas Jack," replied Flo-Flo as she hopped nimbly into the boat.

Nora-Nu picked up the rope that was tied to the front, ran into the surf and leapt into the air. Before she hit the water she had morphed into the beautiful narwhal and dived beneath the waves.

Flo-Flo clapped as the boat tugged about and was pulled easily into the surf with enough force to throw both Alfie and Bampa back into the seats.

After regaining himself, Alfie turned to Flo-Flo and cupping his hands to his mouth, so he could be heard above the gale, shouted, "Nora-Nu said you might ask the wind nicely to calm. Can you actually do that?"

Flo-Flo grinned.

"I could ask nicely, but what would be the fun in that?" the fairy said as she stood up on the bow to face the wind.

"Calm it!" she shouted, her brows coming together in concentration, which soon became a frown when the weather hadn't changed.

"I said, CALM IT!" Flo-Flo bellowed, her face turning crimson.

Alfie held his hands over his ears to protect them from the echoing boom that bounced about the waves. It was the loudest thing he had ever heard.

"It worked," laughed Bampa as a sudden break in the clouds allowed a single ray of sunlight to shine down upon them.

Then as Alfie watched on, the clouds parted to allow light to spread out and as it did, the winds dropped and the waves ebbed away to become glassy smooth.

Flo-Flo nodded her approval as she stepped down into the boat, a smug look on her face.

"That was amazing," Alfie said, taking in the splendid sight of Nora-Nu swimming beneath the surface, moving with long graceful strokes. "I still don't know what I'm supposed to be doing back at Merry Wish, but things seem to be coming together. Hopefully Brother Drum will be as easy to find as you."

"Brother Drum?" Flo-Flo said, her eyes widening as she stared at him. "You mean we are not complete yet? But there isn't much time. Where is he?"

"We don't know. He is hidden from the compass and there are no clues in the journal. Yet now you're found, we can dedicate all our efforts to finding him. I'm sure it won't take long."

"I hope you're right, Alfie Wayfarer. Without all of us here for Christmas, we won't be able to spread the magic. And if that happens, Christmas will cease to be."

10

Brother Drum

"I still don't see why I have to go to school," William said through gritted teeth, his words echoing around the hallway. "Not while all this is happening at home. Surely I should be here helping to find Brother Drum."

"It'll do you good to meet your new class before the school breaks up for Christmas," his father said. "You've only got today and tomorrow. I'm sure you'll be fine. Besides, isn't the shop owner's daughter meeting you at the bus stop? What was her name?"

"Cat," William replied and felt a flush on his cheeks. "But that was before we knew that we had to save Christmas. Isn't that more important?"

"It is important. But so is your education," his mother said, taking William's coat down from the hook and handing it to him. "I want to be here, yet I have to go to work."

William slipped his coat on and grabbed his school bag.

His father smiled as he put an arm around him.

"Listen, I'll come down to the bus stop and meet you when you're finished. Then we can walk through the village and see if we can find some clues as to where Brother Drum is."

"And I'll come with you," Flo-Flo said as she glided down from the steps to land at his feet.

William grinned down at her.

"I can't take a fairy into school with me," he said.

118

"Nobody will see me in your pocket. Besides. Every Wayfarer needs protecting," Flo-Flo replied as she leapt into the air and turned into a sleighbell. William caught her before she fell to the floor.

"Will you be alright inside my pocket all day?" he asked.

The sleighbell jingled in response.

"She said yes," Lola-Bear explained. "And I'll feel much better with a fairy travelling with you. Snogres will be about now that Christmas is almost upon us, and the closer it comes the more snogres will arrive."

"Where exactly do they come from?" his father asked.

Lola-bear shook her head.

"They come with the snow that catches the northerly wind. Yet some are here already. I expect snogres have existed in Samscritch Bay for as long as the Wayfarers have."

"That's a scary thought," his mother said, shrugging into her own winter coat and wrapping a scarf around her neck.

"Have fun," his father said as he walked them to the truck. "You can tell me all about it when I meet you at the bus stop after school."

William nodded and reluctantly climbed into the truck. He hoped the day would go fast so that he could come home to Merry Wish.

As his mother turned the car around and headed through the gate, William glanced at the elf that was perched on top of the fountain. It was in the same position it always was. Maybe he had imagined it winking at him before. Yet as the thought came to him, the elf grinned before sticking out its tongue.

Unafraid of him anymore, William stuck his own tongue out which caused the elf to bark out a laugh, its stone-coloured clothes taking on a hint of green with a subtle hue of red stripes.

He was becoming more real.

Snow slowly drifted down as they made their way along the winding track to the village, his mother was singing along to 'A Winter's Tale' while she drove and he thought he could hear Flo-Flo jingling in time from inside his pocket.

"We still haven't put up a tree," William said, suddenly remembering their own tradition. "Can we do it later? I mean, now we know that Father Christmas is really real, we have to do it."

"I don't see why not," his mother replied as she turned onto the main road and pulled up beside the bus stop. "Cat's already here. That's good. Now kiss your mum before you leave."

"What? No way. Don't embarrass me, Mum," he said as he made a hasty retreat from the truck before she had the chance to lean over and kiss him.

She lowered the passenger side window.

"Good luck today. I'll see you when I get home from work," she said and then looking over his shoulder she added, "Morning Cat."

She was laughing as she pulled away, waving before disappearing around the corner.

William threw his bag over his shoulder and stood inside the concrete bus shelter. He looked up at Cat who had the hood up on her black coat.

"Hi," he ventured, hoping that she wasn't going to be as frosty as the weather.

"Hi," she replied, her dark eyes regarding him for a moment before looking back out into the snow.

"Were you online last night?" he asked, wanting to keep the conversation going. He hated awkward silences. He doubted anyone enjoyed them.

Cat nodded.

"I couldn't find you, though. Thought you might have wanted a game of Duos on Fortnite. Didn't you play?"

"We still haven't got Wi-Fi up at the cottage. There's no internet at all. Not even dial-up," he said, wishing that he had gone online last night. He'd had loved to play alongside Cat on Duos.

He was desperately searching for something else to ask her so the silence wouldn't creep back when the bus pulled up, thick tyres grinding through the settling snow.

"After you," he said, allowing Cat to climb on first.

It was a small minibus with ten or eleven passenger seats. Only two others were occupied. Another girl and boy sat together. The girl looked to be a couple of years older than the boy and with similar pointy noses and narrow chins, William guessed them to be brother and sister.

"Hi," William offered. He got a grunt in response. Both of them going back to staring at their phones.

"Not the talkative type," William muttered to Cat as he sat on the seat beside her.

The driver put the bus into gear and it began to roll again, the sound of snow crunching beneath its tyres.

Cat glanced over at the brother and sister, her eyes narrowing for a second.

"Fatima and Jake Dimwold. Their Dad runs a fleet of fishing boats out of Limerik Harbour. He's a bit of a bully. As are those two. Unfortunately, Jake will be in our class."

"That's not good," William said, glancing over his shoulder and seeing that the pair of Dimwold children were staring at him. Jake's lip curled into a grimace.

"I hate bullies," he whispered as he faced the front, slipping a hand into his pocket and feeling reassurance from touching the sleighbell.

Flo-Flo jingled in response.

"What was that?" Cat asked. "I heard tinkling or something."

William cocked his head to the side as if straining to listen.

"No," I can't hear anything," he lied. "So do we pick up anyone else on the way to school?" he asked, changing the subject.

Cat's frown dissolved.

"No. Most of the children at school come from the other side of the valley. We're the outsiders there."

It wasn't long before the bus turned through the gates of the school and came to a stop between three other busses that were easily twice its length with an upper deck. Children spilt from them in a constant flow, all dressed in school uniforms and heading through large glass doors at the front of the brick building.

William hadn't realised the size of the school and suddenly felt a lump in his throat as his palms began to sweat.

"Come on," I'll show you to the classroom," Cat said, "And don't look so worried. It isn't a bad school," she added as if reading William's mind.

****

"See, it wasn't so bad, was it?" Cat said as he followed her onto the bus and they sat in the same places they had that morning.

"No, It's much like my old school, really," he replied and didn't know why he worried so much.

With the school running down for Christmas, the syllabus was mainly abandoned for light revision and even a few games.

The bus began the journey home, the snow on the ground a little thicker than it was when they had been coming the other way.

He was about to ask her what she was doing over the holidays when he felt a paper ball bounce from the back of his head.

He looked over his shoulder to see Jake grinning at him.

"Hey, new boy. How come you're living in this crappy village? Bet you've got one of those tiny little stone huts right down on the beach," Jake said, his grimace widening as William gripped tighter to the head rest. "What are you getting for Christmas, a new net so you can collect driftwood for your mum?"

"Ignore him, William. Like I told you this morning. He's just a bully," Cat said.

"What was that, Catharine? Sticking up for your new boyfriend," Jake's sister, Fatima, piped in as she leaned closer. "Being the only two from Samscratchy Bay, it'll be up to you to keep the population going."

"Samscratchy, nice one," Jake added as he matched his sister's glare.

William felt Flo-Flo begin to vibrate through his pocket and got the impression that she wanted to come out and teach the bullies a lesson.

Cat spun around and stared them down.

"Actually, William lives in a cottage with grounds that would easily swallow your house up several times over. His father's so rich, he could buy out your father's entire fleet and sink the boats for fun. In fact, that's not such a bad idea. I'll suggest it to him. He's meeting us at the bus stop isn't he?"

William nodded, not sure what was happening but wasn't about to back out now. He wasn't used to friends sticking up for him.

"I very much doubt that," Jake said. "The only large building in this village with any amount of land is Merry Wish. And that isn't for sale otherwise my Dad would have bought it years ago."

"It wasn't for sale because William's family own it," Cat replied as the bus slowed down and stopped. "Take a look at that man there. That's William's father. Now look at the statue in the square, see the resemblance?"

William watched as both Fatima and Jake stared first at his father and then at the statue of his forefather and then back again. He stifled a laugh as their mouths fell open.

"You see, William's father practically owns Samscritch Bay. What do think William? Shall we ask your Dad if he wants to buy out a fishing fleet?"

William grinned.

"Why not," he said as he climbed from the bus, followed quickly by Cat. They watched as the bus pulled away, the faces of Jake and Fatima staring through the window with a look of utter shock on their faces.

"That was class," Willam said and they both burst into laughter.

"What's so funny?" William's father asked as he came to join them, snow had settled onto his shoulders and had no intention of melting.

"Nothing," William replied after sharing a knowing smile with Cat. "See you tomorrow."

"Yep, see you," Cat replied and trudged the few steps to her mother's shop and went inside, closing the door behind her.

"So how was your first day of your new school?"

William kept pace with his father as they ambled across the road and made their way over the village square, leaving fresh footprints in the otherwise pristine blanket. The rest of the village seemed deserted, although lights were on in the pub.

"It was alright."

"Alright? I'll take that as a good sign. Otherwise you'd be whining."

William glanced again at the pub, an idea coming to him.

"Why don't we have a look in there," William suggested, pointing to the thatched building.

His father stopped walking.

"The Broken Compass?"

"Yes. Bampa explained that the toys could be hidden by spirits. What better place than the pub?"

His father stared vacantly at the pub for a moment before his face lit up in a wide smile.

"William," he said, placing a huge arm over his shoulder and squeezing. "You're a genius."

They trudged through the deepening snow to the oak door of The Broken Compass. A wooden sign swung above, showing a portrait of a sinking ship. Not the best image for a sailor to look at before having a drink, he thought.

The warmth from an open fire hit them as they opened the door and stepped inside. The low-ceilinged room was cosy enough, with brasses hanging from exposed beams and black and white pictures on the walls.

"I'll have a pint of your best local ale and half a lemonade for my son," William's father said as he leaned against the bar, having to duck his head to avoid the beams.

"Right you are," said the barmen as he grabbed a glass and began to pull a pint of ale from the tap. Foaming amber liquid ran down the glass, soon filling the pint.

"I don't reckon you've been in here before, but I do recognise you," the barmen said as he placed the pint on the bar and took a half glass down for the lemonade.

"Aye Bert, you'll kick yourself when I tell you," said an old man as he rose from a stool further along the bar. William recognised the old man to be Mr Simon Norris-Ogle. The fisherman he and his mother had met a couple of days ago.

"He's a Wayfarer. Just moved into Merry Wish. Isn't that right?"

William watched as his father's fingers whitened upon the glass as he took a step back from the bar to survey the fisherman.

"Yep, that's right. Just popped down for a quiet drink before heading home," his father said, handing William his lemonade and gesturing for him to sit at a table away from the bar.

William took it and sat near the window, the snow already piling into the corners of the windowsill.

"Merry Wish, aye? A Wayfarer. You're the spit of the statue in the square. There's some strong genes in your family," the barman said, bumping elbows with Norris-Ogle.

"Yeah, We're all good lookers," William's father joked, although William noticed that his eyes never left the fisherman's.

Taking a look at the pictures on the wall, William found that they were of the village dating back over a hundred years, and some of the fisherman pulling in the day's catch, beards wet with seawater. He was scanning over the rest when his eyes fell upon an old picture of the bar. Like the rest, it was black and white and dated December 56. The bar looked much the same with bottles on shelves in the background, and glasses and tankards aligning other shelves, but in the corner, perched in a small alcove was a toy drum – the Wayfarer crest painted in gold on the front.

His heart thumping harder, William searched the bar, standing to see past his father but the alcove didn't have a drum in it. There were only bottles of rum.

When his father came to join him, William nudged his leg with his own and nodded towards the picture of the bar.

"What is…Oh!"

His father glanced back to the bar as William had done but a frown soon settled over his brow when he didn't find the drum.

"Is something bothering you, Alfie?" Norris-Ogle said as he leaned against the bar, cocking his head to one side, a knowing grin sitting deep in his grey beard, "Something in that photo?"

"Well, yes, actually. The drum. My son noticed that it has a sleighbell on. Much like our family crest. In the photo it's behind the bar, yet it's not there now."

The barmen leaned over the bar and narrowed his gaze.

"Aye, I remember that old thing. It was always behind the bar, ever since I was a nipper and my old Dad ran The Compass. I sold it years ago."

"Who bought it?"

William knew his father was desperate to know yet kept his expression neutral.

"Why do you want to know that? If it was sold, it was sold," Norris-Ogle said before throwing the rest of his drink back and placing the empty glass on the bar. "As it happens, I bought it."

"Just curious. It's not often I see the family crest outside of Merry Wish. I was only wondering how it ended up at the pub," William's father said as he knocked back the rest of his pint and stood, his irritation seeming to seep through as he placed the glass down harder than was necessary.

"Funny how things from Merry Wish end up around the village around Christmas time. But don't worry yourself. The drum is safe enough. It's back at home, tucked up nice and tight alongside my prized whisky."

"Come, William. I think we better be getting home," William's father said as he placed the empty glass on the bar. "Gorgeous ale, by the way."

Then putting their backs to Norris-Ogle, they both strode out into the cold.

"Dad. I think that man knows what we're doing up at Merry Wish. And I think he's one of those snogres," William admitted as they began the walk home.

"Your mum and I thought the same the other night when we came to fetch Nora-Nu. I think he's someone we're going to have to avoid."

William stopped.

"He has Brother Drum. We can't do what must be done without him," William said as the pub door swung open and out stepped Norris-Ogle, that sly grin was back on his face.

"Give my best to old Jack, won't you?" he said before sauntering off in the other direction.

Suddenly William's pocket burst into life and Flo-Flo erupted from it, morphing into her fairy form as she flew after the old fisherman.

"Easy, Flo-Flo," William's father said as he caught and wrapped his arms around her.

Flo-Flo struggled, hands balled into fists, her face positively alive with anger while her wings flapped wildly.

"Although, you could follow him. From a safe distance of course. At least we would know where he lives and maybe we could find a way to rescue Brother Drum," William's father suggested.

Flo-Flo stopped struggling as she thought about it, her glower shrinking until she seemed calm.

"I will do this. You must return and tell Lola-Bear and the others what has happened. I'll be back as soon as I know where that snivelling snogre lives," Flo-Flo said.

She leapt into the air and changed into a beautiful bird with a sleek body, dark feathers and a sharp beak.

She ascended into the falling snow, cutting through the veil with ease, soon disappearing into the darkening sky. She cawed once, the sound coming from high above the village.

"That was incredible," William said as he heaved his school bag onto his back. "I can't wait to tell mum."

11

A Fairy Rescue

Flo-Flo stretched her wings to their fullest, gathering the rising thermals as she followed the snogre. The exhilaration of flying flowed through her. It had been decades since she had last spread her wings as a falcon, seeing through keener eyes, flying faster than she ever could in her fairy form. If the worry for Brother Drum and the approaching Christmas hadn't been with her to focus her mind, she would have loved to fly higher. Instead, she watched the snogre as he made his way through the village, casting furtive glances behind him should he be followed. Yet the threat was from above. And even if he chose to look skyward, he wouldn't see her. She was far higher than the old man could see.

Passing a row of cottages, the snogre turned down a narrow footpath which led him to a lone house situated between two ferns. He stopped at the door, looked behind him and then stepped through.

Flo-Flo plummeted from the clouds, racing down faster than sound itself before flinging her wings wide to gather the air and slow her descent. She swooped between the ferns and landed on the snow-covered windowsill.

She transformed back into her fairy form before peeking through the window.

Between the gaps in the drab curtains she saw a small living room with a single chair. There was a coffee table, a television and an open fire. The rest of the room was stark with only a single picture on the wall for furnishings.

"He's not here," Flo-Flo whispered to herself as she opened her fairy wings and flew above to a bedroom window. Again, apart from a bed and a plain wardrobe there was little else. Maybe the snogre was lying about having bought Brother Drum.

A light in the bedroom suddenly came on as the snogre entered.

Swiftly, Flo-Flo flew above and over the thatched roof to the back of the cottage. She floated down past a foggy glass window which must have been the bathroom and carried on to the windowsill of the lower window. Through it she found the kitchen and on the far wall were shelves laden with bottles of whisky. And sitting between two tall bottles was a toy drum.

"Found you."

Carefully, she twisted the handle on the door. She winced as it creaked loudly, but it was locked.

Easing the handle back up she put her mouth to the lock and gently blew through the hole, wishing for the lock to open. A heartbeat later she heard the mechanism turn and the door opened.

Slipping inside, she closed the door behind her and tiptoed across the kitchen to the shelving. She was about to lift Brother Drum from between the bottles when the snogre walked in.

Reflexively, Flo-Flo morphed into a sleighbell and fell to the kitchen counter with a thud.

She would have winced if she had a face to wince with.

Sensing the snogre walk past the counter she willed herself not to be seen, which was easy enough to do when humans were involved, but snogres were a slippery bunch. She could only hope he didn't see her.

Time seemed to stop as she waited for him to leave. What was he doing? As a sleighbell she couldn't see what was going on and could only feel the sounds as they echoed within the hollow of her shape.

A kettle came to the boil and she heard the clink of a mug. A fridge door open and then close. He was making a cup of tea. He hadn't seen her.

Hurry up, she willed him.

Footsteps came past her as they headed for the door, then paused.

"What do we have here?" came the snogre's voice as Flo-Flo suddenly felt large fingers gripping her tightly.

She was about to change back into a falcon and fight back but before she could even think about her next move she was dropped into what felt like an empty jar.

"A sleighbell, aye. With the Wayfarer family crest," came the snogre's voice as Flo-Flo felt the jar rise and tip, her shape rolling around the bottom. "Could it be that I've trapped another fairy?" he laughed.

Flo-Flo attempted to morph into a fairy, but the confines of the jar wouldn't allow it. She was trapped.

"I'm guessing Jack's son sent you to spy. To attempt a rescue of the drum. Ha! Fools, the lot of them."

Flo-Flo felt the jar being carried and then placed down, the glass walls clinking against another glass wall which she guessed to be bottles of whisky. Most probably beside Brother Drum.

Now the compass wouldn't be able to find her. Why hadn't she flown back once she knew where the snogre lived? Why had she tried to rescue Brother Drum alone?

She knew why of course. Lola-Bear had always said she was too adventurous.

"Oh! Christmas tree Oh! Christmas tree," the snogre sang as Flo-Flo felt the ground shake. The monster was dancing. "You'll soon be forgotten. The North will be, the North will be – home to all the snogres."

He finished the verse with a bout of giggling.

"That's right," he continued, flicking the glass with a finger. "Old Nicholas won't be passing above us this Chrimbo. Nope. I can feel it now – the magic is beginning to ebb away. The spirit will be lost and no amount of Christmas cheer will bring it back. But don't you worry. When my brothers arrive, we'll be gentle with the Wayfarers. As gentle as we can when we push them from the heights of Merry Wish cliffs. This time we're going to end the bloodline once and for all."

****

"She should have been back ages ago," Willam said as he paced back and forth in the lounge, Jack was worried he would trip over the carpet and stumble into the fire.

"I'm sure she'll be fine. She's a strong one, Flo-Flo," Jack said as he tried to reassure his great-grandson.

It felt strange coming to Merry Wish a couple of days ago. Feeling the Christmas tingle as he stepped over the threshold, seeing the toys wake up, experiencing the joy of the place. He hadn't known he would miss it so much. Yet now, with Flo-Flo going missing, he realised that the reason why he had stayed away for so long was because of the darker element of Merry Wish.

The enemy.

He believed it was snogres that had killed his father and he was sure they had caused the accident that his son and daughter-in-law had died in.

Jill put an arm around William and guided him to the empty Chesterfield.

"Wouldn't the compass point to her?" she asked, looking to Alfie.

Alfie nodded as he fished the compass from his pocket.

"Great idea," he said as he wound the bevel until it lined up with the image of the falcon. But even from where Jack was sitting, he could see that the needle wasn't moving. It was as if Flo-Flo had been hidden again.

"I hate to say it. I think she has been caught by Norris-Ogle," Alfie said, his shoulders slumping.

Lola-Bear's bottom lip stuck out.

"Oh no! Poor Flo-Flo," she said before turning to hug Nora-Nu.

Jack offered them a smile.

"You can't harm the Christmas fairies. And she's pretty tough," he said as he gripped his cane and rose to his feet.

"Where are you going?" Jill asked as she reached to steady him. But Jack was stronger now. He had been feeling revitalised with a fresh vigour ever since stepping back into Merry Wish.

"I'm going to visit Norris Ogle. I think I can remember where he lives. Let's just hope he's in the same house he was as a boy."

"And I'll come with you," Alfie said as he drove a fist into his palm.

Jack shook his head.

"You need to stay here. This is between me and him. It's been a long time coming. He used to bully me as a boy and he probably had a part to play in my father's disappearance."

"But what are you going to do? I don't think he'll listen to your threats," Alfie said.

Jack chuckled.

"You're right. He wouldn't give a stuff about my threats. That's why I'm taking Lola-Bear."

****

"Are you sure about this?" Jill asked as she brought the truck to a stop beside a narrow footpath between two houses. "If he is indeed a snogre, he could be dangerous.

Jack nodded before climbing out of the truck. He paused before closing the door.

"I've been hiding for far too long. I thought that if I stayed away this whole sorry business would sort itself out. But hiding only seemed to make the problem worse. I need to put a stop to it now for Alfie's sake, for William's sake and for the sake of Christmas itself."

Jill leaned across the seat to take his hand.

"Be careful," she said, then let him go. "I'll keep the engine going."

Jack offered her a smile as he closed the door, then one hand in his pocket, the other on his cane, he ambled along the footpath which he hadn't walked down in over seventy years.

He stopped outside a lone cottage between two ferns and knocked on the door. A light came on from within and an old grizzled face peered at him from behind a curtain.

It was Simon Norris-Ogle. He'd aged all those seventy years yet Jack recognised the high cheekbones and menacing glint in his eyes. It could be no one else.

He disappeared from the window and came to the door. After sliding a bolt he opened it and filled the doorway, arms crossed and wearing a cocky grin that split his grey beard.

"Jack," he laughed. "I thought you'd show your sorry face sooner or later. I suppose that big oaf of a son has come with you, aye?"

Jack narrowed his eyes as he took a step closer, attempting to rise onto the balls of his feet to match Simon's height.

"No. I came alone."

The fishermen stared past him and up and down the footpath and when he couldn't find anybody his grin widened.

"Let's not waste each other's time, Norris-Ogle. You've got a couple of things of mine and I want them back," Jack said, trying to keep his voice even, yet he heard the anger lacing each word.

Norris-Ogle chuckled.

"Do I? As we're not wasting each other's time I can let you know that I bought one of your precious items years ago. And the other stumbled onto my property. But don't worry none. They're both quite safe."

"How about you let me in so we can discuss this in the warmth," Jack suggested. "Perhaps we can come to some kind of arrangement."

"Asking to come into my lair, old Jack. You're feeling a little brave, aren't you? Or maybe a tiny bit desperate."

Norris-Ogle stood aside, allowing Jack to enter the cottage, and then followed him into the living room.

The room appeared large, but Jack realised that was due to the lack of furniture. A single chair sat in front of a television and between them both was a coffee table.

"Well?" Norris-Ogle said as indicated for him to sit in the chair.

Jack lowered himself down and placed Lola-Bear on the coffee table. Her sleighbell form rocked gently before settling still.

"I believe you've got one of these in your possession. I would like it back, along with the toy drum. You don't need such items yet they are valuable to me," Jack said as he produced his wallet. "I'll give you what you paid for the drum and also whatever else I've got."

Norris-Ogle shook his head.

"What do I want with money? You know the reason why I have them and why I can't give you them back."

Jack slowly placed his wallet back inside his pocket and then set his cane before him, grasping the silver handle tightly.

"I'm trying to be civilised, Simon. There's no need for anyone to get hurt. Give me what I came for and I'll be on my way," Jack said.

Norris-Ogle laughed.

"You're an idiot, Wayfarer. Do you think I'd allow you into my home and simply give you what you want?"

Jack stiffened as Norris-Ogle reached behind the curtain and produced a shotgun. He levelled it at Jack's head, a steady hand upon the stock, aged finger resting on the trigger.

"Although, I must thank you for bringing me a gift," he said glancing down at the sleighbell on his coffee table. "It looks like Christmas has come early for me. But I'm afraid you'll never see another one."

Jack looked on as the fisherman's grin widened. His canines growing an inch longer and protrude over his bottom lip like a sabre-toothed tiger's. His forehead began to flatten as his nose stretched into wolf like muzzle.

The beast grew long white hair all over his skin, the shaggy fibres even coming out of its tall ears.

"It's been a while since I felt the need to drop my human disguise. It seems appropriate now, don't you think?"

Jack had only seen a snogre once before when he was little. One that had followed him home after playing in the snow outside the grounds of Merry Wish. It had grabbed him and dragged him to the cliff edge, laughing as it was about to toss him over.

Jack had been too scared to fight back. Terror and shock made him limp like a cloth doll. It was only the timely arrival of his father that had saved him. That and the shotgun that he had brought with him and used to threaten the snogre.

Now, all these years later he was once more being threatened by a snogre, but this time it was the monster that was holding the gun. Yet Jack felt no terror.

"Just remember, Simon. You brought this upon yourself," Jack said and drove his cane upwards.

The cane struck the barrel of the shotgun, knocking it towards the ceiling as it emitted a flash and an eruption filled the room.

Norris-Ogle growled as he brought the gun back down yet there was an eruption of another kind.

Lola-Bear launched from the table, morphing into a fierce polar bear that towered above the snogre, striking the gun away in an instant with a huge paw while barrelling Norris-Ogle to the ground.

"No," he managed to whimper as Lola-Bear stepped over him and lay a huge paw on his chest, pinning him to the floor while she lowered her head to meet his, a rumbling growl filling the room as she bared sharp teeth and roared.

Jack had only seen Lola-Bear in this form once before when he was a boy. It had frightened him then just as it did now. Lola-Bear was a colossus in white fur.

"Please, Jack. Call her off," Norris-Ogle stammered, his eyes becoming large circles. "Please."

"She's not a pet. I won't call her off. However, if you told us where our friends are, she may not crush you," Jack replied, enjoying seeing the squirming snogre. He knew Lola-Bear wouldn't harm anyone if it could be avoided, but Norris-Ogle didn't know that.

"They're in the kitchen. On the shelves. Take them and leave."

Jack rose slowly and left the room, leaving the snogre pinned in place. He made his way to the kitchen and found Flo-Flo in a jar alongside Brother Drum, hidden behind bottles of whisky.

"I've got you, Flo-Flo," he said as he unscrewed the jar and tipped it up allowing the sleighbell to roll onto his palm.

She began to sparkle as Jack placed her on the counter where she burst into her fairy shape, glistening snowflakes cascading all around her as she hugged Jack.

"Careful, Jack – the fisherman of this house is a snogre," she warned, taking a step back so she could reach up and grasp Brother Drum.

"I know. He's in the living room. Lola-Bear has him in hand, or should I say paw."

Flo-Flo let out a joyous laugh, her smile so wide it filled her face.

"Jill's out front down the footpath. Take Brother Drum and meet us there. I've got a few things to sort out before I leave."

Flo-Flo nodded and slipping the straps of the toy drum over her shoulder, she flew out of the back door and disappeared into the night.

Jack returned to the living room to find Norris-Ogle attempting to wriggle from beneath the gigantic polar bear, yet Lola-Bear's paw pressed down on his chest and prevented him from even taking a deep breath.

When he saw Jack re-enter his gaze pleaded with him.

"You have what you came for. Please let me go."

Jack stepped closer, the tip of his cane almost touching the snogre's ear as he leaned down so he was staring directly into Norris-Ogle's face.

"If I see you up at Merry Wish, if you interfere with Christmas, if you so much as sneer at a Wayfarer or any of my kin, we'll come back. This is not a threat or promise, it is a fact," Jack said in a calm and measured voice. "Do we have an understanding, snogre?"

Norris-Ogle nodded, or at least tried to. With Lola-Bear pressing down on him his movements were restricted.

"Good."

Jack stood straight and stepped to the door where he paused and turned back around to take in the image of his enemy, then making eye contact with Lola-Bear he gave a subtle nod.

The ground shook as the polar bear marched after him, the bulk of her body tearing the door frame out of the wall before they emerged into the snowy night.

That will give Norris-Ogle something to remember them by.

By the time they emerged out of the other end of the footpath, both he and Lola-Bear were chuckling. Now in her fairy form they climbed into the waiting truck to find that Brother Drum had been awoken by Flo-Flo.

"Welcome awake, and merry Christmas," Jack said. The drum made several sharp beats from within itself followed by a rhythmic roll which sounded like laughter.

Then laying a hand upon Jill's arm he said, "Take us home. I'm sure the others are sick with worry."

Jill put the truck in gear and they rolled away, leaving tracks in the deepening snow.

12

Following the Journal

Snow fell relentlessly from the grey sky without showing any signs of stopping, adding to the already deepening blanket that covered the grounds of Merry Wish and making high drifts in the walls.

"Be careful. There may be black ice in the village," Alfie warned as he said goodbye to Jill as she was about to leave for work, dropping William off at the bus stop on the way through Samscritch Bay on his final day before the holidays.

"It's me," she replied, laughing. Then kissed him on the cheek.

"Hey, that's my line," Alfie laughed as his wife put the window up and set off through the gates.

The wind picked up as he watched them disappear down the track, causing the fat flakes to swirl before drifting over the cliff's edge where it fell into the sea below. It was beautiful, as was the entire white landscape before him.

As he walked back to the house he passed the fountain where he momentarily paused to brush snow off the elf which was sitting proudly upon the top. The stonework was beginning to take on more colour the closer Christmas drew near. Not that he could see much of it. The elf was currently white with his face hidden beneath a thick coating of snow.

Bampa explained that the elf would remain at his vigil until Christmas Eve, a sentry posted to watch out for threats.

"Not long now," Alfie said to the statue as he swept a hand over the reddening pointy hat and cleared snow that had caught beneath the large pointy ears before wiping the smiling face.

The elf suddenly shook and blew flakes from his eyes before snorting more from his nostrils.

"Better?"

The elf treated Alfie to a wink before his gaze once again settled on the gate, perpetually scanning for any would-be intruders.

Alfie left him to his vigil and sauntered back into the house, stamping his feet on the floor before removing his coat.

"There you are my boy," Bampa said as he stepped out of the kitchen, the journal in hand. "I've made coffee. Bring it in and let me show you what I've found in the journal.

Alfie quickly collected the tray from the kitchen and carried the coffee pot and mugs through to the lounge and set them down on the table. Then relaxed back into a Chesterfield, his grandfather was in the other, leaning closer to show him the journal.

"See this?" he asked, pointing to a diagram sketched into the book. "It's the positions of where the fairies and toys must be on Christmas Eve." I've confirmed it with Lola-Bear already. She, her sisters and the toys all know where they must be for when he comes. Brother Drum will be central, keeping beat."

Alfie absorbed the diagram. It was the sphere-like machine - the anchor - that William had found on their first day at Merry Wish. The picture was in the shape of a compass with each Christmas fairy set at quarterly lines; North, East, West, South, and inlaid between the fairies were the toys, just as they were laid out on the compass which was used to find them. At the centre of the diagram, in the middle of the circle of toys and fairies was the Wayfarer family crest. Bampa noticed him looking at it.

"And here is where you'll be standing, making the tradition complete. Once we're all in position, the way lines will open and Father Christmas will have free reign to travel across the world at star speed, delivering presents to all the children. Cheating time with the help of Brother Drum."

From the corner of the lounge came a drum roll. Alfie glanced up to find Brother Drum perched upon the windowsill, his sticks vibrating upon the skin.

"The snogres will try to prevent us from entering. For if we're not in position on time, St Nicholas won't be able to achieve star speed."

"And the children of the world will be without presents. But if the tradition hasn't been performed in over seventy years, how has Father Christmas circulated the world in a way that beats time?" Alfie asked.

Lola-Bear shrugged.

"I think he still has certain energies stored in the sleigh and the reindeer were pushed harder than normal. Yet mistakes have been made. And the way lines are so weak now that it would be impossible to achieve what must be done without the machine cranking up. That's why Merry Wish called you home, and why we must not fail."

"And we won't," Alfie's grandfather said, striking the ground with his cane for emphasis. "This Christmas is going to be a belter."

"Yes, I can already feel the spirit rising in Merry Wish," Lola-Bear said. "It's been quiet for far too long," then turning her attention back to the journal, she moved her childlike finger and the pages flicked over by themselves.

"This is what we must do next," she said, laying the tip of her finger over a picture of a complex chimney.

"Oh, yes. I remember now. My father had a special ladder for climbing up onto the roof," Bampa said as he rubbed his chin. "Although, come to think of it, I distinctly remember it toppling over and breaking. I don't know where it is now."

"Yes," Nora-Nu said as she floated down beside her sister, eyes gleaming with excitement. "It came crashing down before the last time the anchor was used, smashing into pieces. It was used for firewood."

"Then we will need to make a new one. Or we could buy one I suppose," Alfie suggested, wondering if he could order one online. He probably could, yet the chance of it arriving before Christmas was slim.

"Or," Nora-Nu said, smiling mischievously. "We could fly you up there. Between the two of us, we could carry you."

"I don't know about that," Alfie said as he rubbed his shoulders, the memory of falling from scaffolding a few months ago reminding him how hard and unforgiving the ground could be.

There was a twinkle in Lola-Bear's eyes that gave him a sudden warmth that filled his chest. She, nor the other Christmas fairies, wouldn't let any harm come to him. And if he did perhaps fall, she could always kiss him better.

"Alright. Let's do this," he said and laughed as Nora-Nu skipped into the air and spun several times before landing, leaving a small cloud of snowflakes to drift to the floor.

As they stepped outside, the wind seemed to pick up, a gust instantly gathering around him as if attempting to rid him of his jacket.

"Right, so how are we going to do this?" Alfie asked.

In answer, Lola-Bear and Nora-Nu each gripped his trouser legs and lifted him.

He flung out his arms to steady himself, although it was born more out of reflexes than thought as no amount of arm waving would make him steady.

"Not too fast," he warned as he was lifted over the ornately carved eaves and heaved up the roof to the chimney. He barely had time to raise his hands to prevent his face from planting into the large four-pot stack.

"How does it look?" Lola-Bear asked.

Alfie studied the large chimney. It was one of the biggest he had ever seen and made from flint and lime, which was unusual. The pots themselves seemed to be a kind of pot clay. He gave them all a tap with the knuckle of his finger. Three of them seemed fine, although the fourth sounded dull.

"This pot's got a crack in it," he shouted down to Lola-Bear. "And some of this mortar needs repointing, but apart from that, it looks sound."

He tried to glance down at Lola-Bear without seeing the ground below but failed. It was a long way to go if he fell.

"I've got the tools and some cement in my truck. I can fix it when Jill comes home."

"That is good," Lola-Bear said as she and Nora-Nu lowered him to the ground.

Alfie glanced back up at the chimney as he rubbed the stubble on his chin.

"I'll see if I can find a ladder somewhere. Or at least a hoist that I can strap around the chimney. No offence, but I think I'd do a better job at repointing the stonework if I wasn't held up by two fairies."

Lola-Bear and Nora-Nu laughed.

"Perhaps that's for the best," Lola-Bear said.

"Good. Now let's see what else is in that journal while we have a cup of tea. The snow's coming in again and I've got to walk into the village to meet William at the bus stop later."

****

Alfie zipped up his jacket and pulled the hood over his head, yet stray snowflakes still managed to find a way through to settle and melt against his cheeks and neck. Trying to ignore the unpleasant sensation he marched across the grounds of Merry Wish and out into the pristine white countryside.

There wasn't much else to find in the journal that his father hadn't already told him and so without anything else to do, he decided to head out a little early to Samscritch Bay, just in case the weather turned worse. Not that he would complain if it was snow. He loved it, although, if things turned icy it may become treacherous underfoot, and the last thing they all needed was one of them to get hurt so close to Christmas.

Nora-Nu skipped beside him, occasionally leaping into the air to catch a snowflake in her mouth and then giggled afterwards.

"You try," she said after catching him watching her.

Laughing, Alfie jumped up, opened his mouth and attempted to catch a flake. He failed.

"It's not as easy as it looks," Nora-Nu said before leaping once again and expertly closed her mouth around another.

"No, it isn't," Alfie said. Then changing the subject asked, "Has Samscritch Bay changed much since you were last wakened?"

Nora-Nu's nose scrunched up as she thought about it.

"Not from what I've seen. It's been pretty much like it is now since it was founded. Only the people have changed, and perhaps the arrival of electricity. Although, it does feel a little sadder, a little duller. I think that could be because there's not been a Wayfarer in the village for so long. It'll change after Christmas. You'll see."

"So the way it snows all the time here. Is that because of the strange power that comes from Merry Wish? I mean, the rest of the country rarely gets snow, unless you're up in the moors or in Scotland. Even then, not like this."

Again, Nora-Nu thought on the question.

"Merry Wish is linked to the North Pole, to where Father Christmas lives. I suppose some of the weather may overlap. Like some of the magic."

"Is that why the snogres live in the bay?"

Nora-Nu nodded.

"Snogres can't leave Samscritch. The original ones can't, anyway."

They followed the track along the cliff's edge before cutting across country, heading along a narrow footpath that was barely discernible to the fields on either side of it. Only a row of low hedges marked out the way.

"What do you mean, the original ones?" he asked.

Nora-Nu wafted her wings and began to fly alongside him, leaving a trail of sparkling flakes to mingle with the snow.

"We don't know how they came through, maybe they followed the original Wayfarer when he travelled south to these lands. But it's clear that the magic that binds Merry Wish to the North Pole also binds them. They can never leave, only be sent back. Or killed."

Alfie thought that the last words didn't sound right coming out of a girl that looked so young. He kept forgetting that the Christmas fairies were thousands of years old.

"Like Norris-Ogle?"

"No. I think he was a descendant. He was born in the village. One of his forefathers, or foremothers would have been a snogre. The chances are, he could have left if he wanted to, but chooses to stay. That would be the snogre blood calling to him, keeping him close to Merry Wish."

Alfie must have been showing worry on his face because when Nora-Nu turned to him she smiled.

"It'll be fine. This is going to be the best Christmas Samscritch Bay has seen in almost a century."

They came to the end of the footpath and ambled across the lonely square to the bus stop, Nora-Nu promptly morphed into a sleighbell as she flew towards Alfie who caught her and stowed her away inside his pocket.

He doubted he would ever get used to seeing magic like that. He may have thought more about it but he looked up to find that the bus was pulling into the stop and William stepped off closely followed by Cat.

Alfie waved to them as he made his way across the road. The bus pulled away, leaving a cloud of exhaust fumes billowing behind it.

"Good day at school?" he asked as he took William's bag and slung it across his shoulder.

"It was alright, I suppose," he said, then turning to Cat he pointed towards the shop across the square. "There's no light on, has your Mother closed early?"

Cat shrugged.

"Sometimes she has to nip into Exeter to pick up magazines. Especially when the snow comes in and the delivery truck can't make it out here," she answered. "She would have left the back door open though."

"Are you sure?" Alfie asked, feeling a little worried for her. He wouldn't have left William home alone, but then, this was one of those small villages where people left their doors unlocked. Then dread entered his thoughts as he thought of the snogres that may be lurking around. "Let us walk you to your door at least."

"It's okay Mr Wayfarer. My mother does this all the time," Cat said as she began to trudge away.

"I'd feel better knowing that you got inside. This snow is coming down thicker and there could be ice paths."

Cat shrugged.

"If you insist."

The front of the shop was locked so they made their way down a side entrance which led them to a small courtyard garden to the rear of the property. Squeezing between a shed and bins, Cat stepped onto the back porch and tried the handle.

It didn't move.

"It's locked," she said, wrinkles creasing her brow. "She probably forgot to leave it on the latch before she left."

"Either that, or she thought she'd be back before you but got caught out in the snow," Alfie suggested. "Can you call her?"

Cat took her phone from her pocket and held it to her ear.

Alfie exchanged a glance with William while they waited. He shrugged.

"It's saying her phone can't be reached right now. I'm guessing she's got no signal. It doesn't matter. She won't be long. I can wait here."

"No you can't," William said. "It's freezing. You can come back with us. Dad?"

Alfie nodded. He didn't like the idea of bringing someone back to Merry Wish but he couldn't leave her here by herself.

"Of course, she can. Jill will be back soon, so she can drop you back off in the truck. At least you'll be warm. You can keep calling your mother while we walk, to let her know where you are."

As they set off Alfie got his phone out to call his grandfather. He picked up on the first ring.

"Bampa, we've got a visitor coming. One of William's friends from school," he said, slowing down and lowering his voice so Cat and William wouldn't hear him. "We haven't much choice. It won't be for long. You'll have to warn Lola-Bear and the toys. They'll need to hide."

He slipped the phone back into his pocket before striding a little wider to catch the other two up. He kept silent, letting them talk between themselves about some computer game they wanted to play.

Cat tried her mother several more times before leaving her a message, telling her where she was going and that William's parents would drop her off later.

It didn't take long to make it back, following Alfie's footprints that were going the other way.

"Wow!" Cat said as she came to a stop before the big gates to Merry Wish. Her eyes went wide as she stared across the grounds, taking in the fountain and the animals that were ambling around. The stag was rubbing his antlers along the bark of a tree while the arctic fox looked at them before leaping and diving nose-first into a snow drift.

"This is incredible."

Alfie hoped the elf on the fountain kept still.

"Yeah," William agreed, his face beaming with pride. "There's animals all over the grounds. And we've got a boat house that links to the river which takes us directly to the sea. And we've also got a labyrinth."

"Really?" Cat asked turning to Alfie.

Alfie nodded.

"Dad, can we go to the labyrinth?" William asked, his eyes pleading with him.

"Yes, but don't be long I'll make us some hot chocolate."

Alfie smiled as he watched them both run across the grounds to the rear of Merry Wish, and almost laughed as the elf on the fountain's head turned to follow them, confusion forcing his smile into an upside-down U.

He walked up to the fountain and leaned closer to the elf as the children passed from view.

"It's fine," he chuckled. "She's a friend of William's. Don't go scaring her."

13

Different Snow

William ran around the corner of the house, his feet crunching in the snow as he guided Cat towards the labyrinth.

"This is so cool. I would love to live in a place like this," Cat said, her grin almost as wide as William's. "Have you solved the labyrinth before?"

"Yeah," William replied as they arrived at the entrance. A large stone arch with an elf standing to one side, which he was sure wasn't there the last time. In fact, he was sure it was the same elf who was sat upon the fountain.

How had he gotten around here so fast?

"What's wrong?" Cat asked, her eyes narrowing.

William shook his head.

"Nothing," he answered, but Cat had already tracked his gaze to the stone elf, who was now wearing a scowl.

"Does the pixie thing scare you?" she teased, her hands settling on her hips as she laughed.

"No. And it's an elf," he replied, hoping that she didn't detect the uneasiness in his voice. He wanted to run back around to the fountain to check if it was indeed the same elf. Maybe the Christmas fairies had sent him to watch over them.

He wished he could tell Cat about the magic, about the fairies and Christmas. The secret was beginning to nibble at his nerves and he was sure he would let it slip at some point.

"You know what," Cat said as she rummaged around her pockets and brought out a lipstick. She pulled the lid off and approached the elf. "I'm going to make him less creepy."

Before William could stop her, she leaned in close to the statue and coloured its thick lips in a dark red which stood out starkly against the stone.

"There," she said as she stowed her lipstick away. "That's better."

William slowly approached, wincing as he stared at the scowling elf now wearing a dark shade of rouge.

"I think he looks even creepier," he said and almost jumped as Cat let out a loud laugh.

"Come on, I'll race you to the centre," she said as she ran through the arch, leaving him alone with the elf.

"Wait," he shouted as he ran after her, It's a lot bigger than you think."

He followed her prints as they made a left, then a right turn within the maze and then almost ran into her as she suddenly stopped at a dead end.

William glanced around the high stone walls, trying to remember if the dead end was here when he entered the labyrinth with his mother a few days ago. He didn't think so.

"This way," he said, taking her arm and pulling her back the way they had come. He led her along another wall and turned right before coming to another dead end.

"I thought you knew the way," Cat teased.

"I do, at least I did. This way," he insisted and kept the wall on his left shoulder as he traced his way along another route, turning right and then left while trying not to step into the deepening snow drifts which formed along the bottom of the walls. They made several more turns before coming to a dead end once again.

"You're right. It's a lot bigger than I thought it was," Cat admitted as she stepped closer to the stonework and drew an arrow with the lipstick, back the way they had come. "If we mark which way we came from, it'll be easier to find our way back."

William slowly nodded while his mind was trying to work out why he couldn't find his way around. It seemed like a totally different maze than the one he and his mother had solved. Perhaps it was the snow that covered everything that made it all look the same.

"Let's go this way," Cat suggested as she took his hand and led him back to the walls they had left but instead of turning, they carried on through a gap before swinging right.

William tried to concentrate but all he could think about was how warm Cat's hand felt in his and hoped that she wouldn't let it go.

"Oh, another creepy elf," Cat said as they rounded a corner and came into a square area which was a crossroads. The elf was standing at the square's centre, arms folded and wearing a scowl.

"Wait," Cat said as she took a cautious step closer to the stone statue. "Look at its lips. It's wearing my lipstick."

Not wanting to let go of her hand, William stepped with her but as her words sunk in he froze. Had the elf followed them?

"It can't be," he laughed attempting to pull her away.

"Yes. Yes, it is. Look," she demanded, wiping a finger along the elf's lip and showing him the fingertip where it was smudged with lipstick. "How is it here? How is it even possible?"

Her eyes grew wide as she looked back at the statue. "What's going on?"

William desperately searched his mind for an excuse but the elf chose that moment to grin, its thick lips spreading from pointy ear to pointy ear.

Cat gasped, her fingers digging so painfully into William's that he gasped himself. He wanted to tell Cat that it was alright. That the elf wouldn't harm them. That in fact he was there to protect them, but contradicting him before his words were even out, the elf lunged for Cat.

"Run," he shouted as he took off down one of the paths, pulling Cat after him.

He spared a glance over his shoulder as the elf chased after them, eyes narrowing with determination as long fingers reached before it.

"This isn't real," Cat demanded as they made turn after turn before coming to a dead end. "And look at that," she said pointing to the floor where their own footprints seemed to pace right through the wall. "The walls have moved. We're trapped."

"Dad!" William shouted as loud as he could, but his words seemed muffled as they hit the stonework. It was as if the labyrinth soaked the energy out of them. "Daaad!"

"Quick, this way," Cat growled as she pulled William out of the dead end and down another path, the elf still chasing them, its stone feet clip-clopping over the cobbled floor, a relentless pursuer from another world.

"Why is it chasing us?" Cat asked as they made more turns.

"I don't know," William said as they emerged into another crossroads. Not another, he soon realised, it was the same. He recognised their prints in the snow.

"Which way?" Cat demanded as she frantically looked around, a scream escaping her as the elf emerged from around the corner they had run from.

"I don't know, let's try down here," he shouted as he ran in the opposite direction from the elf, grasping Cat's hand and pumping his legs for all they were worth.

They took several more turns before emerging into a circular space with a bench at its centre.

"We've reached the middle of the maze," William said as they darted around the rear of the stone bench to put a barrier between them and the elf which entered the circle after them. It slowed as it realised they were trapped, its snarl slowly becoming a grin.

"Stay back," William warned as he frantically looked around for something to use as a weapon.

"What is it?" Cat asked as she gripped tightly to his arm,

"It's a Christmas elf. A real one," William admitted, wondering what he could tell her. But since the stone creature had come to life and was chasing them, he couldn't deny what they were both seeing.

"Christmas elf? They're not real," she said, eyes never leaving the advancing statue.

They watched as it stepped closer to the bench, its head bowing down as if looking for something on the floor before it pressed its boot into the snow.

An audible click emanated from where it was standing, followed by a whirring of gears and the bench suddenly dropped away to reveal a large circular hole, a tunnel which led down at a steep angle like a slide at a water park.

The grin on the elf widened as he pointed a long finger at Cat and then down at the hole.

"No. I'm not going down there," Cat said as they backed away, but the walls around them began to close in, bringing them forward and closer to the gaping hole.

"Dad" William tried again, yet the sound was more muffled than it was before.

Panic was setting in as he glanced around for a way out but there were none and with the walls shrinking around them, they were running out of options. The walls even seemed to be growing taller so climbing out was no longer possible.

Cat let out another scream as the elf lunged for her and closed long fingers around her wrist, pulling her away from William.

"Get off her," William shouted as he gripped her hand tighter and pulled her back, but the elf was stronger.

His feet slid in the snow as he was dragged with her, the elf guiding Cat towards the hole.

"Let go of me," Cat cried as she slapped and tore at the stone hand which bound her. She kicked at her attacker's shins yet the elf didn't appear to notice.

"No, no, no," she yelled, each word growing louder as her feet slipped over the hole and she began to slide down, falling backwards and flinging out a wild arm.

William caught it but the snow had melted on her sleeve and the fabric slipped through his grasp and all he could do was watch as Cat slid out of view, her scream becoming more distant until it disappeared altogether.

"What have you done?" William said, turning on the elf who stepped away, wringing his hands in defence. "Where does it lead?"

The elf didn't answer, only beckoned him away from the hole.

The grating sound of whirling gears began to turn once again and William noticed that the walls were beginning to move back and the hole began to shrink.

"Cat," he shouted.

He gave the elf one last glance before diving through the hole head-first, landing on his belly and began to slide down.

He glanced up to see the worried look of the elf staring back at him, its head swiftly becoming a silhouette as it shrank from view.

"Cat?" he shouted as he rolled onto his back and then swung his body round so he was travelling feet first, the slide becoming steeper as he gathered speed.

Darkness engulfed him as the hole above closed completely, shutting him in the strange slide tunnel that ran beneath Merry Wish.

What could it possibly be?

The tunnel suddenly bent around, making his stomach lurch before it bent back, his body rolling one way and then the other.

Attempting to slow down, he pushed his hands into the smooth surface but they quickly became hot and he removed them before he burnt a layer of skin from his palm.

The slide was made from marble or polished stone, the sides so smooth that there was no seems at all.

He was about to shout Cat's name again when he noticed a light from below. A pinprick of white in the darkness that was slowly getting bigger. No brighter than a faint glow, he drew closer without any sign of slowing.

Then all at once his body felt nothing below him and he spilled out into a never-ending abyss.

He opened his mouth to scream but before any sound past his lips he slammed into a snow drift that swallowed him whole.

For several heartbeats he did nothing. His mind went over the last few minutes and attempting to comprehend what had happened.

How could he have landed in the snow miles under the ground?

Dizzy with disorientation he tried to move but couldn't. He was wedged in tight.

Holding his breath, he began to wriggle, working his way backwards like a worm. He felt his body flop out when hands grabbed him by the shoulders to yank him out the rest of the way.

"William. What in white hell just happened?" Cat said as she pulled him up straight.

William stared at her. She was covered in snow from having landed in the same drift he had.

"I don't know," he said, blinking flakes from his eyes so he could take a better look around. That's when he realised that the slide they had come down wasn't there. It was as if it had simply vanished.

Turning on the spot he saw nothing but a pristine blanket of white in every direction. Snow stretched as far as he could see. Above, stars filled the night. More stars than William had ever seen before as there was no man-made light to blot the night.

"Where are we?" They both said together, their breaths visible as they spoke.

William hugged himself. The temperature had dropped dramatically and his teeth had begun to chatter.

Everything felt wrong. The air seemed empty. Dry. He sniffed and had the strange sensation that something was up his nostrils. He'd felt that only once before, years ago when his parents took him to Lapland. The temperature had been -25c and his nostril hairs had frozen together.

No wonder he felt cold.

And the snow was also different.

He knelt and picked up a handful, squeezing it in his hand, trying to make a snowball but it wouldn't stay packed. Instead, it crumbled into fine powder, much like the snow they had in Lapland.

Then he glanced up at the stars once again and his knees buckled.

"What is it? William?" Cat asked as she caught him, her gaze following his.

"I know where we are," he said, shaking his head to clear his mind as he pointed up. "That's the North Star. See? That one by itself between the frying pan and that W-shaped formation."

"So? I've seen stars before," Cat said, shaking her head.

"But look at it. It's above us. Directly above us."

Cat's brows rose.

"And?"

William clambered to his feet, his gaze never leaving the star.

"If it's directly above us it can only mean one thing. We're at the North Pole."

Cat's mouth fell open.

They stared at each other for a moment, neither of them able to say anything. The silence around them seemed to close in until William thought he had lost his hearing.

"I'm dreaming. I have to be. We can't be at the North Pole," Cat said, turning around to stare out at their surroundings again. "I mean, there's nothing here. Just snow, snow, and more snow. This is ridiculous. How do we get back?"

William couldn't disagree. This felt incredibly surreal to him and he already knew about the elf and the magic that existed within Merry Wish. It must be a strange experience for her.

"Wait, what's that in your pocket?" Cat asked as she pointed at his jacket.

William looked down to find that his pocket was vibrating wildly. The motion growing stronger.

"Flo-Flo," William said as he reached inside to retrieve her.

Cat peered closer.

"What's a Flo-Flo?" she asked.

"Ok," he began, wondering how best to explain it, but thought, there's no other way than the truth. She'd already seen the elf and travelled down the slide to the North Pole.

"Flo-Flo is a Christmas fairy. One of three, actually."

"Really?" Cat said, folding her arms.

He opened his hand to reveal the sleighbell which sat innocently on his palm. A moment later she burst into her fairy form, scowling at the world around them as she hovered in place, her wings beating too fast to see.

To her credit, Cat didn't scream.

"Christmas fairy? Why not, we've already had a stone elf. Wait, you knew about this?"

William shrugged. He may as well tell her everything. It wasn't as though she wasn't involved now. And in a way, he felt relief at finally being able to share the secret with someone other than his family.

14

A World Of Endless Night

Alfie watched his wife drive through the gates of Merry Wish and park near the fountain. A reindeer paused from grazing on lichen from the bark of a tree to momentarily bow its head to her as she climbed from the truck and came over to wrap her arms around him. The arctic fox looked up as he ambled along the drive, took one look at the pair of them before leaping into the air and dived nose first into the snow.

Alfie couldn't help but laugh.

"Miss me?" she asked.

"You know I always do," he answered, placing a kiss on her cheek. "Just to let you know, we brought Cat back to the house. She was locked out and we couldn't leave her. It's okay, though. Everyone's on their best behaviour. The toys are all upstairs."

Jill nodded as they made their way to the entrance.

"Where's the elf gone?" she asked, nodding back to the fountain.

Alfie hadn't noticed he was missing.

"I don't know. He might be on patrol or doing a perimeter check or something. The first time he left his post though."

"Perhaps Bampa or the fairies know. And where is William and Cat now?" she asked.

"They're in the labyrinth. We came back about half an hour ago. I hope they haven't gotten lost."

Jill laughed.

"No, William found his way around it the last time we were in there easily enough. They'll simply be playing."

"You're probably right. It'll do him some good having a friend over. Wait, there's the elf. What's he doing?" he said, letting go of Jill as the elf emerged from around the corner, waving to get their attention.

"I don't know, but he looks worried," Jill replied as they waited. "Is that lipstick he's wearing?"

He slumped before them, attempting to speak but no words left his mouth. Flustered, he thumped himself in the chest and forced a large clod of snow from his throat.

"That's better," he said in a high piping voice. Then returning his attention to Alfie he continued.

"Forgive me, Master Wayfarer," he said, tears beginning to fall from his overly large eyes. "Young William has gone down the shoot. I tried to stop him but he jumped after her."

"What shoot," Alfie began, an anxious feeling creeping up his back. "Are they ok? Where are they?" he asked while fighting the feeling of dread which was rising within him.

Bampa appeared at the door, Lola-Bear and Nora-Nu to either side of him, all wearing masks of concern.

"The trap?" Lola-Bear asked as she flew closer.

The elf nodded before burying his face in his hands.

"I...I thought she was a snogre and was here to steal secrets. That's what I've caught them doing before. And when she drew paint on my lips I knew for sure. She was mocking us, Master."

"What trap?" Jill demanded. "Take us there."

They followed hastily after the elf who was running ahead, his pointy hat bouncing from his head and seeming more real than before, as if the more he was animated the less stone-like he was.

They turned several times in the maze before arriving at the middle where a simple stone bench was at the centre.

"Where are the children," Jill asked again, worry thick in her voice.

The elf pointed at the bench as he stamped down hard on the ground. A moment later a loud grating sound rumbled from below and the bench sunk into the floor to reveal a hole.

"They went down there," he said, pointing at the opening.

"Where does it go?" Alfie asked, staring into the darkness and wondering why William would have gone willingly down there. "Is there a secret room beneath the house?"

His gut clenched as he caught the look Lola-Bear and the elf were sharing.

"No," Lola-Bear said, shaking her head. "It leads to the North Pole."

"What?" Jill demanded as she knelt beside the hole, anger echoing around the maze. "How is that even possible? No, let me guess, it's magic."

Alfie glanced up to see his grandfather approaching with Nora-Nu by his side. Like the rest of them staring into the hole, his face was full of worry.

"Is it true? Have the children gone down the snogre trap?" he asked.

The elf paused his hopping on the spot long enough to nod before he carried on the nervous hopping.

"You knew about this? That there was a trap in the maze that can take someone all the way to the North

Pole?" Jill asked, beginning to pace around. Alfie tried to stop her with an embrace but she threw him off. "That's my son down there, and that poor little girl. How are we going to get them back?"

"I'll slide down with a rope," Alfie suggested, wondering if they had a rope. Perhaps he could use the one on the back of his truck.

"It doesn't work like that," Lola-Bear explained with a grave look on her face. "The slide goes to a different place every time and disappears once the snogre has been evacuated. At least Flo-Flo is with them."

"But they were not snogres," Jill shouted, throwing up her arms in disbelief. "They were children. I'm going to get them back."

She pushed her hand into the hole but it was propelled back by an unseen force. She tried again, leaning her entire body weight against it but couldn't put a single finger beyond the invisible barrier.

"Jill, leave it. You can't go down there. Maybe I can," he said turning to Lola-Bear for confirmation. The fairy nodded.

"Those with Wayfarer blood can pass through."

He stepped closer, knelt and gingerly pushed his hand through the hole. It went through unhindered.

"Wait, how are you going to get back?" Jill asked. "And what are you going to eat? Are there polar bears there or snogres? You'll need provisions."

She hastily left them there while she ran back to the house.

"Will there be snogres and polar bears?" Alfie asked as he watched his wife pass out of earshot.

Lola-Bear nodded.

"They'll be both. And it will be cold. And dark. There's no real sunlight this time of year. Just a continuous night."

"It was like that in Lapland," Alfie said then turned to his grandfather. "The chimney needs repointing and there's a crack in the pot. If we're not back in time, you and Jill will need to fix it so the anchor machine will work."

His father put a heavy hand on his shoulder.

"Leave it to us. And don't worry about Jill. She's stronger than you think."

Alfie knew Bampa was right. Yet it didn't stop the worry from gripping his stomach and squeezing, and that was on top of his son being lost in a frozen wilderness thousands of miles away from home.

Jill soon returned with a large backpack. She was out of breath as she dropped it at his feet.

"There's spare clothes for both you and the children, and food and a pan. There's other things I've thrown in but my mind is all over the place at the moment and I can't think straight, I'm, I'm…"

Alfie hugged his wife tight, feeling her heart hammering through his chest.

"I'll bring them back. I promise."

He kissed the top of her head before putting enough room between them to throw the backpack over his back. The pan that was clipped onto the side with a karabiner banged loudly.

"What am I going to tell Cat's mother?" Jill suddenly said, her hand going to her mouth.

Alfie sighed. What could she say?

"You're going to have to tell her the truth. We can't lie about her child. And a problem shared is a problem halved."

Jill nodded.

"You still haven't said how you're going to get back."

"I'll sort it out when I get there. First I'll find the children and then I'll work the rest out," Alfie said, putting a comforting arm around his wife. "We'll be back before you know it. I promise."

"I'll go with you," Lola-Bear said, then put her hand on Nora-Nu's shoulder. "You must stay here and help with the preparations. Christmas must still happen."

Nora-Nu hugged her sister before taking Jill's hand to lead her away from the hole.

"We will. It'll all be ready for your return," she said.

"Yes," Bampa agreed. "Be careful my boy. We'll keep things going here. You'll find a way back, you're a Wayfarer."

Alfie hugged him and his wife, placing a kiss on her cheek before sinking to the ground and pushing his legs through the hole. Lola-Bear climbed onto his lap as if she were a child climbing onto her father at a slide in a water park. Alfie might have laughed under other circumstances.

"I'll see you soon," he said, offering them a smile before edging forward and then pushing himself off the ground and into the darkness.

He glanced up at the shrinking light and the silhouette of Jill which rapidly disappeared from view until he and Lola-Bear were totally swallowed by the darkness.

Alfie's belly lurched as he felt himself being dragged down, the hood on his coat filling with air like a kind of shoot but it did nothing to slow their descent, only annoying him as it vibrated wildly, bashing against his ears.

The slide bent several times, the gravity force pinning them to the smooth surface while turning them in all directions. He was about to ask Lola-Bear how long the ride lasted but all of a sudden he felt nothing below him as they emerged into a world of white and then he hurtled into a blanket of fresh snow.

Shaking the dizziness from his head he looked around to find that Lola-Bear had opened her wings and was gliding gracefully down to him, making circles in the air before landing.

"I'm in the North Pole," he said, his breath coming out in a huge white plume.

A quietness surrounded him. No movement, no wind, only peace. Then the reason he was there caught up with him.

"I don't see any footprints," he said, searching the snow around him. "I'm guessing William and Cat came out somewhere else," Alfie suggested as he took in the surroundings.

They were in the middle of nowhere. The ground was white, the sky was full of stars and apart from a scattering of fern trees, there was nothing else – except the cold. There was an abundance of that.

"I don't even know where to start looking," he admitted as he pulled his hood tight over his head and pulled the zip up as far as it would go.

Lola-Bear helped him to his feet and brushed snow from his trousers.

"If I was Flo-Flo I would start to make my way to the North Pole."

"Why? What's there? A scientific research centre?"

"No. Father Christmas of course. It's the only place around here that might offer shelter. Where there'll be food and warmth."

"Alright. Good. Then we've got somewhere to head at least. I only hope that's where the others are heading."

Lola-Bear slowly turned in the air, staring out at the horizon while sniffing, her nostrils flaring.

"There. That way," she said, pointing away from them.

"Are you sure? It looks the same no matter where you point."

The fairy nodded while tapping her nose.

"Christmas has a certain smell, a fruity, spicy, piney sweet smell. It's not strong but it's definitely there. Follow me."

Alfie trudged after Lola-Bear, having to take as wide a stride as possible as his feet disappeared into the deep snow. The heavy backpack didn't help. If only he had snow shoes this would be a lot easier.

"How long until we get there?" he asked, realising that he sounded like a child on the back seat of a car.

"I don't know. Maybe a day, maybe two. Depends if the weather changes. If a storm comes in we won't be able to do anything other than dig a hole and wait it out."

"Then let us hope we don't hit a storm," he said, but no sooner had the words passed his lips than the wind picked up.

15

Lost

William was on the second verse of 'Oh Holy Night' when Cat suddenly stopped and he walked into the back of her.

"What is it?" he asked, staring over her shoulder as she slowly turned to face him.

"Your singing. That has to be the fifth time I've heard you sing that song since we set out. I've endured three 'Oh Holy Nights', six 'Oh Christmas Trees' and several renditions of 'Jingle Bells'. I'm stopping you before you begin 'The Twelve Days of Christmas' for the third time."

William shut his mouth as she stepped closer.

"This is your fault that I'm here, so please – no more singing."

William held his hands up.

"I'm sorry. I sing when I get nervous."

"I like it," Flo-Flo said as she floated beside them. "No better way of keeping the spirits up than singing Christmas cheer. Come on, there's a storm coming in and I want to be in that tree line before it hits."

Flo-Flo began to fly ahead, pausing long enough to beckon them on.

"We better do as she says," William said as he stepped level with Cat.

They had been walking in single file so they could step in each other's footsteps to avoid them both having to wade through the snow, taking it on turns at leading. It was now his turn.

"And I promise not to sing," he added.

"Sorry. I didn't mean to snap. I'm not adjusting well to all this," Cat admitted, waving a hand about them.

William had to agree. And the cold didn't help. Not that it seemed to bother Cat. He trudged on, pushing his feet through the white powder and dragging the rest of his body after, lurching on the best he could without toppling over.

Ahead, Flo-Flo began singing 'Silent Night' and giggled as she glanced back at Cat who must have been frowning.

"Where do you suppose she is leading us?" Cat asked.

"I don't know. To the pole, I think," he said and then stopped.

"What is it?" Cat asked.

William slowly turned to face her, resisting the urge to grab her hand. "You know who'll be there, right?"

Cat shook her head.

"Father Christmas."

William felt himself grinning and didn't care. Flo-Flo had to be leading them there. Why else would they be heading to the North Pole?

"Don't be daft," Cat said as she strode past him. "He doesn't exist."

"No? Hours ago you didn't believe in Christmas fairies, yet here we are following one. And I've already explained about what is at Merry Wish. Trust me, he is real."

The wind picked up, driving snow horizontally across the open wilderness and peppering them both with an icy chill.

William hugged his coat tighter around himself and jammed his hands into his pockets.

He'd never been this cold before.

"Come on, we better get into the shelter of the woods before we're buried out here," Cat said as she grasped William's arm and trudged on. William was only too happy to oblige, his heart hammering from the exertion, or was that from the contact with Cat?

The night grew darker as they ducked beneath the tall spruces, the ground a rolling blanket of needles and roots feeling soft underfoot. William was glad he was no longer wading through the deep snow, his calves and thighs were burning from the effort of keeping up with Flo-Flo.

Sound travelled differently inside the woods where the wind could no longer bite at them. Instead, the trees themselves groaned as they swayed as if trying to talk.

"Where's she going?" Cat asked as they stared after Flo-Flo who was weaving between the branches and burghs of the spruces, quickly vanishing from view.

"Hey, wait for us," William called after her as they began a jog.

The ground was easier to cover inside the woods, although they needed to keep low and even duck at times to avoid the lower branches which grabbed at them as they traversed the roots and dips.

"Flo-Flo?" he called after her but she had gone.

"What do we do? We can't keep going if we don't know where she is. We could easily get turned around in the woods and not know which way to go."

William nodded as he slowed to a stop.

He turned around on the spot but every direction looked so similar that it wouldn't take much for them to be lost. In fact, he wasn't sure which direction the Christmas fairy had gone.

"Flo-Flo," he bellowed, his voice coming back to him in an echo.

"The important thing to do is not to panic," Cat said as she attempted to hide the panic. She'll come back. You said she was sworn to protect you, right?"

"Yep."

The upper branches of a spruce close to them suddenly rustled and a large falcon burst through, its wings spreading wide to slow it down before it landed.

Cat gasped as it turned its head towards them, its sharp beak spreading wide before snapping shut.

"It's okay. This is Flo-Flo," William explained as the falcon morphed back into the fairy and offered Cat an apologetic smile.

"Sorry for startling you. I needed to fly up high to get a grasp of where we are," she said, her cherub face taking on a solemn look. "And although I now know where we are, it isn't the best of news."

William shared a glance with Cat, feeling immense guilt for having gotten her into this.

"We're either a single night's walk in that direction to the North Pole or a three night's walk going around the forest."

"Then the obvious choice is through the forest," Cat said.

"Yes, but it's also the more dangerous. We're in the glacier forest, home to the snogres. I'm not sure we could pass through undetected."

"What's a snogre?" Cat asked. "Like a polar bear or something?"

"No, nothing as pure and beautiful as a polar bear," Flo-Flo explained. "They're snow ogres."

"Huge monsters with tusks, claws and sharp teeth," William added, raising his hands and holding his fingers as though they were large claws. "I've seen pictures of them. Maybe we should take the safe route and go around the forest."

Flo-Flo nodded her approval as she began to step away from them and headed out in a different direction.

"No, wait," Cat said, glancing the other way. "I still think we could cross through and arrive in one night. I mean, we haven't got any provisions. No food, tents or spare clothes. three nights out in this is simply ridiculous. What if we were really careful?"

William thought that she had a point. What would they do without food? And three nights of walking in the snow seemed like torture. And Christmas was only two days away.

Flo-Flo stared between the pair of them until her gaze settled on William.

"The choice is yours. You're the Wayfarer. The path must always be yours."

What would Dad do? He wasn't scared of anything. But then he heard his Mother's voice in the back of his mind telling him to be sensible. And the sensible and safest choice would be to go around the forest.

"I think we should go through," he said and returned the smile that Cat was giving him.

Flo-Flo shrugged as if she wasn't surprised by the choice, although she didn't look too happy about it.

"Then we shall press on. I only advise you to be quiet. And if we see any snogres, run," Flo-Flo said before skipping deeper into the forest, slipping between low branches and over-exposed roots with ease.

It grew darker the further they went, the canopy of the trees blotting out the sky almost completely, forcing them to walk with hands held out before them to catch any branches that might strike them in the face.

They stopped often to rest, melting snow in their hands to drink while Flo-Flo glided above the trees to make sure they were heading in the right direction.

"Will there be elves?" Cat asked as she rested against a thick trunk. "You know, like the one that forced us into the trap."

William shrugged.

"I think so. But that was a soldier elf. A guard. I don't know why he made you go down the hole. I'll make sure I tell Father Christmas what he did."

"Didn't he make you go down the hole as well?"

"No, I went down to help you. I didn't know what was down here and couldn't bare the thought of you coming down alone."

Cat shoved her hands into her pockets and glanced away.

"So you had a choice?"

"Yes. There was no way I was going to stay up there with the elf. He scares me," William said and froze as Cat came towards him, a strange look on her face. He thought she might thump him but instead she hugged him.

"That was sweet," she said.

William hugged her back, feeling his face flush with heat. He never felt like the hero type before. He still didn't.

"Come, we've still many more miles to go," Flo-Flo said as she swooped down, interrupting them. "And be watchful. Snogres are a sneaky bunch."

They plodded on, William's legs now aching with fatigue but not wanting to admit it while Cat was marching easily in front of him, seeming more at home in the frozen wilderness than he did. She didn't even appear to be cold whereas William felt like his face might crack if he pressed his cheeks too hard.

"Stop," Flo-Flo suddenly said as she held her hand up.

William and Cat halted and ducked.

"Wait here," the Christmas fairy ordered before morphing into a bird and flying silently ahead.

"Do you think she's spotted snogres?" Cat asked as she peered above the roots they were crouched within.

"I hope not. I don't think we could fight one."

"Can you smell that?" Cat asked, her nostrils flaring.

William sniffed the air. The smell wasn't one of his strongest senses but he was definitely catching a hint of smoke.

"Fire?"

Cat nodded.

"Cooking. I can smell a stew or something," she said as William's stomach growled loud enough for Cat to hear.

"We haven't eaten anything since school dinner. I'm starving," she complained. "Come on, let's take a look."

Before William could hold her back, Cat crawled forward and edged over a small crest.

"Cat?" William whispered as loud as he dared. Then crawled after her.

As he neared she beckoned for him to come up beside her and keep low.

Shuffling awkwardly he manoeuvred onto his belly and pulled himself level so he could peer over the side of the crest.

Below them was a small clearing with a fire burning at its centre. Above the fire was a cooking pot with a steaming broth inside. William may have gone further to investigate if it wasn't for the two large creatures that slumbered beside it.

Larger than his Dad, they were covered in a white pelt and had large horns sprouting from the tops of their heads. They curled back like the horns of a goat. They also had tusks that protruded from their mouths like a wild bore. One of them sniffed the air and snapped his head around to glare in the direction they were hidden in.

For a moment, William thought they had been spotted. He held his breath until the monster's attention was brought back to the cooking pot.

"We better crawl away," William whispered.

"Are those snogres?" she asked as they slowly edged away.

"Yeah. At least that's what they looked like in the journal."

Once away from the crest they flopped back into the roots they were hiding behind as Flo-Flo returned, changing quickly back into the small fairy.

"Be quiet or you'll both be in the stew," she warned, pointing the way ahead. We'll need to turn back. It's too dangerous."

"Can't we simply go around them?" William asked as he saw Cat's scowl deepen.

"You're the Wayfarer, William. But if there's one camp here, there'll be many more in the area. And not all of them will be cooking."

"Perhaps we ought to go the long way round. Better to arrive late than not at all," he whispered.

"That will take us even longer now that we've already been walking for ages. Can we at least try to skirt around them?" Cat asked.

William looked from Cat to Flo-Flo and back again. He hated being the one to have to choose.

"We could at least try. If we hit any more camps or snogres we'll turn around. But I think it's worth one more go," he said and knew he had made the right choice when Cat's face lit up with a smile.

Then just as quickly, it vanished. Swiftly becoming a mask of terror.

"Look out," she said as Willaim felt something slam down on his hood and grip him tightly before wrenching him from the ground.

His world spun as he was pulled about so quickly that all he saw was a blur of white and green, the image of Cat's horror-struck expression embedded in his mind before the wind was driven out of him as his body hit something hard.

When his vision stopped spinning he found that he was on the shoulder of a huge beast and being carried rapidly away from Cat who was hiding behind a tree. She came back into view as she charged after him, shouting his name.

He tried to scream at her to stay where she was but he was struggling to breathe and the bouncing gait of his attacker knocked any remaining air from in his chest.

Kicking his legs he tried to turn around, but he was pinned, a thick arm gripping him tightly, an arm covered in white fur, just like the bare feet that were hitting the ground beneath him.

It was a snogre.

"William," he heard Cat scream as she ran after him, but she was slowly losing ground. For all the size of the snogre, he moved through the forest as fast as a racehorse.

He caught a flash of movement as Flo-Flo swept over him, her falcon form clattering with the snogre's shoulder as sharp talons dug into the white fur.

The snogre came to a stop, growling as he swatted at the bird, his claws missing Flo-Flo by a hair's width, yet the Christmas fairy fought on, scratching and biting with her hooked beak until inevitably she was caught with a backhand which sent her reeling into a tree trunk.

"Flo-Flo," William shouted as he watched the falcon strike the hard bark and slip down into the snow.

He was desperate to go to her and see if she was injured, but the snogre gripped him tighter and ran through the forest, his shoulder digging into his stomach with each loping stride.

16

A Snogre Revealed

Jack leaned on his cane as he stared up at the chimney, the crack in the pot standing out from the ground, and even the sinking sun couldn't hide it.

"How are you with heights?" he asked, turning to Jill who stared up with her arms folded and her collars turned up against the wind.

"Heights, I'm fine. Mixing cement, not so much. And I doubt I'd do a good enough job at repairing it. Maybe we should hire a local builder. At least they would have scaffolding and the expertise. I'm sure it would only be a half-hour job for somebody with experience."

"You're probably right. But you won't get anybody this side of Christmas. Especially from the village. They're mainly fishermen."

Jill continued to stare, her eyes watering from the cold, or most probably from the recent events.

"They'll be fine, you know. Alfie and the children," Jack said. "They'll be back before you know it."

Jill nodded while checking her watch.

"I know they'll be fine. They have to be. But they've been gone for hours now and Cat's mother will be worried sick. I have to tell her. I just don't know how."

Jack caught movement from the corner of his eye and found that the elf had sprung to attention on the fountain and was glaring out at the gates.

Jack's heart began to beat faster when he saw who was approaching.

"You better get inside and fetch Nora-Nu. This may get ugly," he said as he gripped his cane and clambered towards the gates, the elf marching ahead and rolling his sleeves up. The large stag joined them, its head down to display its formidable antlers.

"I told you to never come here," Jack growled through the gates.

Norris-Ogle gripped the bars and leaned so close his nose almost touched the metal.

"Aye, but that was before you took my granddaughter hostage. Where is she? Where's Catharin?" he demanded.

"Cat is your granddaughter?" Jack asked, a final piece settling into a puzzle. That's why the snogre trap was sprung in the maze.

"Well?"

Jack sighed, wondering how to handle the situation but it was Jill who took control.

"You better come in," she said. "Is Penny with you?"

Norris-Ogle shook his head.

"No. My daughter-in-law is up North, visiting her sick mother. I'm taking care of Catherin for the next few days. She doesn't know about any of this. And neither does Catharin. So, I'll ask you again, where is she?"

Jack stood aside to allow the gates to swing inwards and the stag slowly backed away, his antlers still remaining on target should the snogre suddenly attack. The elf needed a nod to step out of the way, his glower told him that he was ready to spring on a heartbeat.

"She wasn't taken hostage. We would never do that. Not to anyone and especially not to a child. She was locked out and so William offered to take her home until her mother could come to collect her. It was an innocent mistake."

"Aye, Penny said she got a text from Catherin saying as such. But she shouldn't be here. I'm taking her home. What? Why are you looking at me like that?"

"Why don't you come inside and I'll fix us a cup of tea," Jill suggested, stepping towards the house.

"Or something stronger," Jack added.

Norris-Ogle grabbed Jack's arm and spun him around, almost pulling him off his feet.

The elf moved in and grasping the fisherman's hand, squeezed and twisted it around his back, forcing a yelp from Norris-Ogle.

"Get that thing off me. All I want is Catherin and I'll go," he said through gritted teeth.

Nora-Nu appeared at the door, her wings fluttering as she flew closer, a long unicorn horn appearing in her hand and seeming extremely sharp and deadly.

Jack held his hand out to stop her before things went too far.

"If you calm down, the elf will release you," Jack said. "Attack me again and I'll let Nora-Nu take you out into the bay and drown you. Do you understand?"

Jack didn't like to use harsh words in front of Jill, but he thought they would be the only ones that Simon would understand.

Norris-Ogle gave a single nod and pulled himself free, rubbing the wrist that had been twisted.

"Cat isn't here. She's," Jill began, her brow crinkling as she sought the right words. "She's at the North Pole."

Norris-Ogle opened his mouth to speak, his scowl deepening to the point of looking painful.

"The North Pole? How do you expect me to believe that?"

Jill shook her head.

"I don't. I'm still having trouble believing it myself. Believing all of it, really. Yet it is the truth. My son as well. They went down the trap together."

"And now we know why," Jack added. "The trap was meant for snogres. If she's your granddaughter she'll have snogre blood in her."

Norris-Ogle ground his teeth and appeared angry enough to thump him. Jack readied himself for the attack.

He couldn't blame him. If it was the other way around and William was missing, he would probably do the same. But it seemed that Norris-Ogle calmed himself, letting go a deep breath.

"If it was a snogre trap, why had your grandson fallen into it?"

The elf stepped closer, raising his hands in frustration.

"The young Master followed her down the shoot. He went to help," he said, his thick lips trembling as a tear rolled down a cheek.

"And how are you going to get them back?"

The elf shook his head, gripping his hat in frustration.

"There is no way back."

Norris-Ogle gripped the elf's jacket and hauled him off his feet, shaking the small body which was half his size.

Nora-Nu slipped her unicorn horn between them, the point resting below Norris-Ogle's chin.

"Put him down, Snogre. This tragedy was nobody's fault. Hurting the elf or any of us will not bring your granddaughter back."

Norris-Ogle opened his hands and let the elf fall to the ground. He instantly crawled to Nora-Nu before standing back up, his glower towards the snogre quickly returning.

"So what do we do? We can't leave them there."

"My son went down after them. He'll bring them back."

Norris-Ogle shook his head.

"How? Unless he can charter a plane from the northernmost point on Earth, how is he going to bring them back?"

Jack rubbed his chin, wondering how to explain the plan but the disbelieving look that Norris-Ogle was giving him said that he had worked it out for himself.

"No. They can't. Catharin can't. It goes against everything that we stand for."

"Simon, it's the only way. Believe me, I wish they hadn't gone. But the only way they can return is with *him.*"

Jack recognised the frustration in the other man. A man that he had known for over almost eighty years.

"He is the reason why snogres have been here for all this time. He brought the curse down upon us. The thief stole our lands. He is my enemy. He is my people's enemy. Him and those damn elves."

Jack felt the elf flinch but touched his arm to hold him back.

"Your differences are with the elves. Not Father Christmas, and not what he stands for. And you need to put them aside for Catherin's sake, if not your own."

Norris-Ogle stared up at the sky,

"We were friends once," Jack continued, holding out his hand. "We can be again. I'll understand if you don't want to help. But please, don't try to stop us."

Norris-Ogle stared at the hand, a snarl playing across his lips but slowly it disappeared and the fisherman grasped it.

"My priority is my granddaughter. What must be done to bring her home?"

Jill sighed but it was Nora-Nu that spoke.

"The anchor machine must work in order for Father Christmas to come to Merry Wish. It's going to be tricky without the others here but not impossible. Come, we've a lot of work to do."

The Christmas fairy beat her wings and flew through the door leaving a trail of snowflakes behind her.

Jack slapped Norris-Ogle on the back.

"Welcome to Merry Wish, Simon. You don't happen to have a set of tall ladders do you?"

"Aye. In my shed at home."

"Good. We're going to need them. Oh, and are you any good at repointing chimneys?"

17

Rescue

Alfie put his head down and bent low against the wind that battered at him, spraying him with fine snow which stung as if it were tiny stones. His mind was on the children and hoped they were faring better against the brutal weather. They were both clever and resourceful and with Flo-Flo with them he was sure they would be fine.

His foot caught against something hard beneath the snow and he stumbled forward, catching himself against a tall spruce which drove the wind from his chest.

"Are you hurt?" Lola-Bear asked as she floated down beside him, her cherub-like face showing concern.

"No, I'm good," Alfie reassured her as he pushed himself up straight. "I think I tripped over a root or something.

"They'll be a lot more roots inside the forest, as well as snogres, so be careful," she warned as she set off again, leading him deeper into the woods.

At least, he thought, the wind wouldn't be as biting with the trees catching it.

"Do you think they will be heading to Father Christmas? Do they know the way?" Alfie asked for possibly the third time since they had travelled down the shoot from Merry Wish.

"It's what I would have done. And Flo-Flo knows the way as well as I do. With any luck they'll be there already. It's at the centre of this forest."

"I'm sorry. I can't help but worry. Do you think they would have avoided snogres?"

Lola-Bear shrugged.

"There's no point in worrying about it. The snogres wouldn't be expecting them. Wait, I hear something."

"Is it them? William!" Alfie shouted but as Lola-Bear suddenly morphed into a polar bear with her sharp teeth on display, he knew that she suspected something else.

"Wait here," she said and then bounded further into the forest, her huge white body soon becoming lost amongst the snow.

Alfie crouched low and slid beneath the branches of a pine, but his backpack got snagged and as he tried to wriggle free he caused the entire tree to rock and creak. He couldn't have made more noise if he tried.

With a final wrench, he pulled himself from the tree's clutches and fell to his knees followed by a load of snow which dumped on top of him.

"Brilliant," he said sarcastically as he brushed it from his face and rose back to his feet. He was stamping life back into his legs as Lola-Bear returned, her large body waddling through the trees.

"Did you find anything?" he asked as she approached.

Lola-Bear said nothing. She stopped, her eyes glaring at him before she sniffed the air. Then without taking her gaze from him, she rose onto her hind legs and growled.

That was when Alfie realised that it wasn't the Christmas fairy, but a wild polar bear which looked extremely hungry.

Alfie froze. Fear held him in place. With his mind on children. the extreme cold, exposure and the snogres, the thought of the wildlife had escaped him.

The bear lurched closer, seeming to gain height as he growled into the night. Its paws were huge, the claws which protruded from them looking exceptionally sharp and lethal.

Quickly, he tried to think of what he was always told about how to react to a bear attack.

He knew that you shouldn't run. Bears were as fast as racehorses on land. Or was that rhinos? It didn't matter anyway. He wouldn't have time to run. And climbing a tree was out of the question. He knew that bears were good climbers.

Alfie raised his arms out wide and shouted as loud as he could, his throat burning with the effort. He didn't know what he was shouting. It was no word that belonged in the English dictionary but he didn't care. He doubted the bear would understand anyway.

He thought the trick might have actually worked as the bear paused and cocked its head to one side like a quizzical dog. Yet as abruptly as it stopped, it began to pace again, large canines protruding from its muzzle.

So he couldn't run, he couldn't climb, and shouting didn't work. Alfie reached around the back of his pack and fumbled for the pan which dangled from a karabiner. He caught it and unclipped it before gripping the handle tightly and wielding it like a bat.

A pathetic weapon against such a beast. But maybe all he needed to do was strike it hard enough to let it know that he wouldn't be an easy snack.

Swallowing the fear which gripped him, he raised the pan above his head, ready to swing it at the bear's nose when from behind his attacker came another bear.

"Great," he hissed between his teeth. One bear was bad enough, how could he fight two? Then he noticed that the new arrival didn't act like the first.

Its roar erupted all around them, scaring the birds from the trees and dislodging snow.

The first bear dropped back onto all four paws before turning around, its teeth showing as it faced the new threat.

"Be careful Lola-Bear," Alfie shouted as he slowly backed away, the pan still held before him for protection.

The bears circled each other and now that they were close, Alfie saw that Lola-Bear was easily half the size again of the wild beast, her coat was whiter and her teeth longer. Yet Alfie didn't know if she could fight a real bear. He still remembered her as a small girl.

The wild bear suddenly swiped, long claws narrowly missing Lola-Bear's head as she ducked beneath it. It roared angrily before swiping again, its paw whirring in the air.

If the strike connected, as big as the Christmas fairy was in this form, the damage would still be horrendous.

The wild bear reared up onto its hind legs as it stomped closer to the other, reaching as if about to drop its full weight onto her, but Lola-Bear matched the ferocity, raising up on her own hind legs before colliding with her attacker. The large bodies coming together like a clash of titans.

The ground shook as the giants fought. Each snapping at the other, teeth gnashing together with thunderous claps as they pushed and butted.

Snow filled the air as trees were knocked and the ground was churned up in the frenzied maelstrom.

Alfie backed behind the thick trunk of a spruce and watched as the bears collided once again, the head of the smaller coming down to bite on the large's shoulder but before teeth could pierce flesh, Lola-Bear gave a mighty shove which sent the wild bear toppling back where it lost its footing and fell to the floor.

It slid for a couple of metres before coming to a stop.

Slowly it rose, and sniffed the air but Alfie could tell that the fight had left it. With a sorrowful roar it backed away before turning around and lumbering off.

"That was amazing," Alfie said as Lola-Bear turned into her fairy form. "Are you hurt at all?"

"No. She was only a cub. Poor thing must have been hungry," she replied as she stared after the retreating bear.

"Hungry? I think she was hoping that I would fill her belly. Are you sure she was only a cub? She was huge."

"Yes, now come. We better be gone from here. The noise would have attracted snogres. They're likely to show up soon."

Alfie clipped the pan back onto his backpack as they hastily stalked away from the ground, his heavy boots crunching through the snow.

They continued heading north for the rest of the day – or night as days in the Arctic barely lasted for two hours – without seeing anything.

"I think we ought to rest for a while," Lola-Bear suggested as the clouds above began to clear to allow the stars to once again rule the sky.

Alfie shook his head.

"If William and Cat are out here, I don't want to stop. They might be close. If we stop we could miss them."

"Well, you are a Wayfarer. I suppose we could go a little further. But I don't want you getting exhausted."

"Thank you," he said and began to trudge on once again. "So, you were there in the beginning. With my ancestor, the very first Wayfarer. What was he like?" he asked, hoping that a conversation might keep him going.

Lola-Bear smiled.

"He was kind, inquisitive, and was always asking questions. And a lot of fun. A lot like you. I think it's a family trait. I think it's what makes you, you."

"And you've known every Wayfarer after him. All my forefathers?"

"Everyone of them. And William will turn out the same, I'm sure…shh. I hear something."

Alfie stopped where he was and ducked low to the ground. He hoped it wasn't the polar bear coming back for another try.

"Something is coming," she whispered as she crouched beside him. "I'm not sure what it is."

Alfie stared ahead, and saw nothing at first, but then caught a glimpse of movement. It was small yet darted out of sight as quickly as he saw it.

"I think it's a bird," he said, then yelped as he was grabbed from behind.

In his haste to turn on his attacker he lost his footing and fell onto his back. He struggled with the backpack, feeling like a turtle that had been turned over. He kicked his legs as he righted himself and came face to face with the person who grabbed him.

"Cat?"

"Mr Wayfarer? It is you," Cat replied as she helped pull him to his feet before hugging him. "How did you find us?"

Alfie caught movement from the corner of his vision and saw a large falcon swoop down to Lola-Bear before quickly turning into Flo-Flo.

"Where's William," he asked as he hugged Cat back, his eyes searching the trees for his son.

Cat's lips drew tight before she cleared her throat.

"They have him. They came out of nowhere and just grabbed him."

"Who?" Alfie demanded, his guts clenching with fear.

"Snogres," Flo-Flo answered as she came to land beside Cat. "Earlier today. There's a camp not far from here. That's where they've taken him. We were planning a rescue. I don't know, maybe find a polar bear to lure close to scare them and snatch him back in the confusion."

"What? And how would you lure them?" Alfie asked. "Use yourself as bait?"

He was expecting them to say they had devised another method but from the way Cat shrugged and wouldn't meet his eye, knew that was exactly what they were going to do.

"Look, it's okay. We'll get him back," Alfie said, more to reassure himself than the others. He couldn't let anything happen to William. "It's a good plan. And it just so happens that I know where we can find our own polar bear. One that won't eat us."

Cat glanced around the woods, a scowl crinkling the bridge of her nose.

"Where?"

In answer, Lola-Bear morphed into the huge white beast she was earlier that day.

Cat fell back and landed in the snow, her face suddenly becoming pale as she stared up at Lola-Bear.

Flo-Flo grinned.

"There's nothing that scares a snogre more than a polar bear," she laughed. "Come, let us show you where they're keeping William."

Alfie pulled Cat to her feet and tried to keep his worry at bay. It would do no good to think too much about the plight of his son. Yet the more he pushed the thoughts away the stronger they came back. He couldn't help but imagine that William was in some kind of cave or cage with bars. That he was cold, hungry and alone.

"Are you sure they wouldn't harm him?" he asked for the fourth time. "Would they know that he is a Wayfarer? Would they hurt him if they knew who he was?"

"Shh," Flo-Flo said as they crept over an icy gully, the uppermost layer of water was frozen thick enough for them to walk across, but Alfie could hear the flowing current beneath.

"We're nearly there. And no, they haven't harmed him," the fairy explained.

He already knew that. She, along with Cat, had explained how they had followed the snogre from a distance until he arrived at the camp. It was a simple fire and a small hut. There were three snogres and William had been locked in the hut. Unharmed.

"They haven't, but that doesn't mean that they won't," Alfie protested as Flo-Flo once again put her finger to her lips and signalled for them to crawl.

"It's over that rock," she said, pointing to a large grey boulder that sat in a bend in the gully.

A smell of roasting meat hit Alfie's nostrils and he could make out a tendril of grey smoke as it rose above the rock.

"Follow me and keep quiet," Cat said as she crawled to the boulder, following the bend.

Alfie slipped the pack from his back and crawled after her, the fairies close behind.

Slowing his breathing he slid around the rock and knelt beneath a fern that's branches covered them in a natural shelter.

Ahead was a small clearing. A fire was at its centre, an animal, possibly a rabbit, had been skinned and was slowly been turned on a spit. A large snogre was turning the handle, its eyes locked on the food.

On the further side of the clearing was the hut. It wasn't much bigger than a shed, but made from thick logs. It appeared strong. He supposed it had to be all the way out here. Above the door were bars and through them William peered out.

Mercifully he seemed unharmed. In fact, his attention was solely on the fire and the meat that was cooking above it.

Alfie fought the temptation to rush over to the squat building and fling open the door to rescue his son. Yet knew that they might only have one chance. Besides, he didn't know where the other two snogres were.

He turned his head to speak with Cat and the fairies but they were gone. He caught them slipping back the way they had come and were frantically gesturing for him to do the same.

Alfie felt the snow beneath him shift. He glanced down to see two dark eyes blink from beneath the white powder. Quickly followed by two huge arms that wrapped around his midriff.

The snogre that had been sleeping, camouflaged amidst the white powder, lifted him off his feet and began to carry him towards the fire where his companion began to chuckle, the large canines jutting from his mouth seeming extremely sharp and dangerous.

"Two humans in the same day," one said to the other as he dragged Alfie towards the hut. He lifted a plank of wood which barred the door, opened it and shoved him inside.

"Dad," William shouted as he wrapped his arms around him. "What are you doing here?"

The door slammed shut and the bar was put back in place.

"I came to rescue you," Alfie said as he hugged him back. "Although, I think we both need rescuing now."

18

Clash of the Snow Beasts

William bit down on the chocolate bar that his father had given him. The flavour instantly filled his mouth. He let it sit on his tongue for a while, enjoying the sensation as it slowly melted. It was as if he had never had chocolate before. He'd appreciate it more from now on.

"How was Mum? You know, after you realised I had gone missing."

Alfie glanced down from the window, where he had been staring out since he had been thrown into the hut.

"She's worried, of course. But you know how she is. She managed to get me a pack together, along with supplies. She's always been the practical one. She's now helping Bampa back at Merry Wish. They have to do all the preparations for when Father Christmas arrives."

"Yeah, I bet she's got it all sorted already," he said, tucking the scarf his mother had packed into the neck of his coat. He hoped Cat was keeping warm, although he knew that she didn't feel the cold as much as he did.

"I don't know why the elf chased us in the labyrinth. It was scary, and Cat must have been petrified. We both were."

"The elf came to find us the moment you disappeared. He thought Cat was a snogre. The trap only works on them. I don't know, it must have malfunctioned."

"Cat's not a snogre," William said, hugging himself. Staying still for too long had let the cold seep into his jacket. "Surely as Wayfarers we would sense it. And why are the snogres so against Christmas anyway? It's not like it hurts them or anything."

"Oh! but it does," came a booming voice from outside the door.

William's father jumped back from the bars as a huge head filled it, large teeth protruding through.

"Christmas is a mighty pain to us snogres, especially those damn elves." he continued, his claws gripping the bars as his yellow eyes glared down at him. "And now I know you're Wayfarers I can destroy the bloodline and purge Christmas from these lands forever."

William rose to stand with his dad at the back of the hut, although he was sure that if the snogre chose to, he could still reach them. Or even open the door and step inside.

"Why?" William asked and was quickly shushed by his father who put his arms protectively around him.

"Because you stole our lands. Stole our trees, our animals, and our way of life. For hundreds of years we have had to fight to live alongside those insufferable pointy-eared creatures with their horrible singing and tinkling bells."

"You've been at war all those centuries over songs and bells?" William's father asked, puzzled.

The snogre snorted.

"Just songs and bells he says. You've no idea the pain it causes us. Those sounds pierce our very souls. We cannot settle, we cannot live as snogres should. Our lives have been turned upside down and we've been made to suffer. Yet it is the world that shuns us, calls us the enemy, makes my kind out to be the evil ones when it was the Wayfarers that stole our lands and caused all the misery."

William glanced up at his father who slowly shook his head.

"But why come go Samscritch Bay? Why try to destroy Christmas."

The snogre narrowed his eyes.

"Because we won't get our lands back until Christmas disappears. Until the Father of Christmas has gone. Only then will we have peace. And it will start with the pair of you. That's two generations more that Father Christmas won't be able to anchor himself to Merry Wish," the snogre laughed, his belly bouncing against the door and making it shake in the frame. "And with you gone, that means the line of Wayfarers will die out too, and with it, Christmas."

William's father stepped closer to the door, his hand curling into a fist as if he would hit the monster on the other side, but the snogre had already left, his laughter following him.

"He's not really going to kill us, is he dad?" William asked as he hugged himself. It suddenly felt a lot colder in the hut.

"No. he won't be killing us. Nobody will be doing any killing. He's only trying to frighten you. Wait, I think I see something," his father said as he stared through the bars. He had been keeping vigil ever since being locked up with him. "Yeah, I'm sure that was Flo-Flo flying into that fern over there."

He looked down at him, determination firming his lips.

"Be ready."

William nodded back, although he didn't know what he had to be ready for.

A death curdling roar suddenly cut through the forest, echoing around the trees and rocks.

"Polar bear!" one of the snogres shouted and William heard footfalls running into the camp, followed by heavy breathing.

"Polar bear," the snogre repeated through breaths. "It was right behind me."

"It's not there now," said another. William was sure it was the one that had been threatening them.

"That will be Lola-Bear," his father whispered.

William wanted to get a look and so wriggled between the door and his father.

Outside the hut, the three snogres were staring towards a rock, eyes turning wide as a huge polar bear lumbered into view, its teeth glistening in the starlight as it snarled.

The snogres backed away, claws held high as they attempted to keep a space between them and the threat. The leader, the one that only a moment ago was laughing, darted a look towards the hut, narrowing his eyes.

"Let us leave. The bear will finish the Wayfarers off for us," it growled before turning and running away. The other two followed, not even looking back.

The polar bear gave chase and was soon out of sight, yet her growls could still be heard.

A moment later Flo-Flo flew from behind the rock, quickly followed by Cat.

"Hurry. It won't take them long to realise that they were tricked," Flo-Flo said as Cat lifted the wooden beam which was held against the door and pulled it open.

"Thank you," William said as he stepped out of the hut and was embraced by Cat.

He suddenly felt hot in his cheeks as he fumbled to hug her back.

When she let go he caught his father grinning at him which somehow made him blush more. He might have said something to him but Lola-Bear returned, this time in her fairy form.

"Come, we better get going," she said and led them away.

They kept to a fast pace, Cat and himself having to run to keep up with his father and the fairies. It wasn't easy running through the deep snow. He found that he was catching himself from falling every few steps, as did Cat. They were thankful when they slowed to a swift amble.

"Hungry?" his father asked as he brought out two more chocolate bars and handed him one and the other to Cat.

They marched in relative silence. Flo-Flo flew ahead, her sleek falcon body darting between the branches of the spruces and ferns. Now and again the wind gusted up a flurry of snow from the ground to throw into them, but the night was mercifully clear.

"Is it much further?" Cat asked after finishing her chocolate bar.

Lola-Bear smiled at her. "Not far now," she replied as Flo-Flo returned, landing in her fairy form with a widening smile which filled her face.

"I can see it," she said excitedly. "Come on."

She led them through the trees to the edge of the forest.

Before them, the land slipped away to reveal a white expanse that seemed to go on forever. The northern lights glowed above, a shimmering curtain of greens and blues which swayed to the Earth's magnetic current.

"It's beautiful," Cat remarked, her face full of wonder.

"It is that," Alfie agreed. "But apart from the night show and the huge desert of snow, I don't see anything. Is Father Christmas's village hidden beneath?"

"No, It's there," Lola-Bear said, pointing directly ahead. "You're just not looking right."

Not looking right? William couldn't think what she meant. He couldn't see anything else but the northern lights and snow. Where one stopped, the other began. There was only a blurry shimmer between.

Yet as he watched, the blurry shimmer took on a different shape.

What he first thought was a large snow mound gradually focused into a building. The longer he stared at it the more focused it became, revealing more and more details.

The building had a tall slanting roof, the material hidden beneath a blanket of snow. The walls were wooden, interlocking at each corner where woodland animals were intricately carved. A warm light glowed from within the many windows but they were too far away to see inside.

Beyond the large building were others. A small village hidden beneath the snow.

"Is that where Santa lives?" Cat asked, her eyes wide with wonder.

Lola-Bear nodded.

"It's the busiest time of the year for Father Christmas, especially as Christmas is only a day away. Yet I'm sure he'll find the time to meet us.

"Wait, a day away? Christmas is tomorrow?" William asked.

"Yes. We've spent two nights in the north already. Without any daylight it's hard to keep track of time. But I'm sure Father Christmas will find time for us," Flo-Flo said.

"He'll have to," Alfie said. "He's our ride home."

William took his gaze away from the village long enough to look at his father.

"Ride home? You mean, we'll get to ride in his sleigh. With the Reindeer?" he couldn't help the excitement causing his last word to rise in pitch. Would they truly be riding with Father Christmas?

"Unless Santa has a private jet hidden in his village, I don't see how we're going to be home in time to make sure the anchor machine is working," his father replied.

They followed Lola-Bear as she flew ahead, but after only a few steps Cat paused.

"What's that noise?"

William cocked his head to the side and listened. He couldn't make anything out other than the wind, then he caught a fragment of a rumble and as he listened it got louder.

"It's coming from the forest," he said as he looked back the way they had come.

Suddenly a loud blast from a horn erupted from the tree line and hundreds of white furry bodies pushed through the spruce and ferns.

"Snogres," his father shouted. "Run!"

19

The Father of Christmas

The horn blasted several more times as the snogres came on. They emerged from the trees and poured down the rise.

Alfie could only stare as they rushed towards them. Huge white beasts that blended with the pristine white powder which they ploughed through, their fur becoming almost one with the environment.

He put an arm around both the children and steered them away from the threat and towards the village.

He pushed them ahead of him as he floundered over the snow, his legs sinking too deep to do any more than lurch, his backpack swinging and clattering against him, almost knocking him off balance.

He quickly slipped his arms through the straps and let it fall behind him. If the snogres caught them, he doubted he would have any need of it.

"There are thousands of them," Cat shouted as she and William struggled to keep up with the fairies. Although younger and more agile than himself, they were a good deal shorter and could only manage a strange jumping stride with arms flailing as they kept upright.

Alfie glanced over his shoulder and wished he hadn't. The snogres were gaining on them. He could see their breaths coming out in great plumes of vapour, see their teeth, their wild eyes full of hate. And above all, he could see that they were gaining on them.

"Keep moving," he shouted as he pushed the children on, yet as he straddled the next bank his foot sank deeper and he went down face-first into the snow.

"Dad?" William shouted as he yanked on his arm.

"Don't stop for me, keep going."

He pushed himself back onto his feet and struggled on, half hopping and half running. He didn't look back, he couldn't. He was sure the snogres would be right on top of them.

Maybe he could slow them down and give his son and Cat a chance to make it.

No sooner had the thought come to him than Lola-Bear turned back, morphing into a polar bear as she came to stop by the children.

"Climb up," she ordered, her teeth bared towards the approaching threat.

"Quickly now," Alfie urged as he lifted first Cat and then William onto Lola-Bear's back. "And hold on tight."

The great bear bounded on, the children gripping to her fur as they bounced on her back. Alfie followed at a better speed now he could place his feet in the paw prints left behind them.

Without thinking he looked back and yelped.

A monstrously large snogre was bearing down on him.

It was bigger than the rest, its legs longer and thicker and so was able to gain on him.

Alfie was about to turn to defend himself when there was an ear-piercing shriek and Flo-Flo darted across his vision and flew into the face of the snogre.

"Don't stop," she warned as she flew in tight circles around the beast, easily avoiding his swatting arms.

Gritting his teeth, Alfie turned and began to run for all he was worth, the cold air hitting his face, driving deep into his chest. They just might make it.

A trumpet blast piped from the village and hundreds of little elves came running from around the buildings, racing towards them.

Alfe hoped they were not going to prevent them from entering, but as they neared he could see that they only had eyes for the snogres. They raced past Lola-Bear and the children, large candy canes raised as they spread out to form a wall, then slammed the candy canes into the snow.

The moment Flo-Flo had flown past them the candy canes brightened and a red and white shimmer flickered along them, forming a translucent wall.

The approaching snogres slowed to a stop, but the bigger monster couldn't halt in time and careered into the shimmering barrier.

There was a flash and the snogre flew back, arms and legs flailing before he hit the ground. When he sat up, Alfie could see that parts of his white fur were singed, which seemed to make him look fiercer.

"That was amazing," William said as he and Cat slid from Lola-Bear's back before she turned into a fairy.

Alfie could only agree with him.

The elves spread further, the shimmering red and white barrier spreading with them until it reached around the entire half of the village. And as he watched he could see that the light had risen above them to become a dome.

As he joined the others, four of the elves approached, each carrying a candy cane which was cocked onto their shoulders as if they were ready to use them.

"Lola-Bear, Flo-Flo? What are you doing here?" one of them asked. His red and green uniform had three snowflake pips on the lapels and his pointy hat had a large C on the front.

"Hello, Captain Nibbly. Thank you for rescuing us. These are our friends. There was a mix-up back at Merry Wish and, well, here we are."

"A mix-up at Merry Wish? So these are Wayfarers?" he asked, staring up at Alfie, William and Cat."

He took a low bow, as did the rest of the elves. When he stood again, he was grinning from ear to ear.

"It is an honour to meet you. There hasn't been a Wayfarer here in, well, not since the beginning. And a very Merry Christmas to you all. Now, I take it you're here to see Father Christmas."

Alfie was about to say yes but it was William who beat him to it.

"Yes. Santa, Yes," he said jumping up and down excitedly, but paused once he saw that Cat was laughing at him.

"That would be great, thank you, err, Captain Nibbly," Alfie added, feeling the excitement pouring off his son.

"Then follow me, please. I'll escort you there myself. Let us hope that he hasn't already set off."

Captain Nibbly marched through the village and the elves followed behind them, smiling and waving to others that came to the doors of the buildings or were peeking out through the windows. All were full of joy and were happy to see them.

"The spirits are high as we prepare for this evening. Yet we're all busy, especially Father Christmas. It happens every year. We think we're fully prepared but come Christmas Eve and we always find ourselves rushing around at the last minute," Captain Nibbly said.

"Always," laughed Lola-Bear as she skipped ahead holding hands with Flo-Flo.

Alfie could only nod as he soaked in the scenery. Every single tree was decorated with colourful lights and baubles which glittered over the snowy ground.

They came to a large building in the centre of the village. Pristine snow clung to the ornate roof and intricately carved shingle which swept down to round windows. Green and red bunting hung between the eaves and golden lights were suspended from each corner.

"This way," Captain Nibbly said as he led them up a short windy path to the front door. The knocker was in the shape of a sleighbell and clanged heavily against the solid wood.

"I can't believe we're really going to meet Santa," William whispered as he bobbed up and down on the balls of his feet.

"Mee too," Alfie admitted as his cheeks began to ache from all the grinning he was doing. He couldn't help himself. The mood in the village was infectious.

The door swung in, letting out a golden glow of heat and silhouetting a large man.

"Oh, Alfie Wayfarer. I wasn't expecting to see you here," said a kindly voice as he stepped into the light.

Lola-Bear and Flo-Flo immediately flew into him and wrapped their arms around his neck.

"We've missed you," they said together.

The man was of a height with Alfie, with round shoulders and a rounder belly. Gentle blue eyes peered at him through round-rimmed spectacles which he pushed up a round button nose. He was dressed in red trousers, with red braces over a green vest.

"And I see you've brought young William too," the man continued, his lips all but invisible beneath a bushy white beard.

"How does he know your names?" Cat asked, cocking her head to stare up at the man.

"Because he's Santa," William answered without looking away. "He knows everybody."

Father Christmas laughed, his belly wobbling as he looked to Cat, then he stopped, puzzlement wrinkling his rosy cheeks.

"Not everybody. I don't believe we've met, child. What is your name?"

Cat stared up at him, her lips tight before she answered.

"I'm Cat Norris-Ogle. But you wouldn't have met me before. I don't think you've ever visited my house."

"You're who now?" Alfie said, wondering why William had never mentioned it. "Are you related to Simon Norris-Ogle?"

"He's my grandfather."

Alfie glanced at Lola-Bear who was now staring at Cat with wide eyes.

"Then the trap in the maze didn't malfunction. You're a snogre," he said.

The Captain hissed before issuing orders to the elves around him who instantly brandished their candy canes and surrounded Cat.

"I am not one of those monsters," Cat said as she backed away from them, her hands held up before her. "I'm not a snogre."

"No, she isn't," William said as he stepped between Cat and the elves. "She is with us. She's my friend."

"That's right, Father Christmas. Cat is with us. She is from Samscritch Bay," Alfie said, half of him not believing he was speaking with Santa, and half of him wondering how he could return the children home if Father Christmas refused to help now that one of them was a snogre.

"This would explain why I don't know your name, young lady," Santa said as he took a step onto the porch and put a gentle hand on her shoulder. "I know it now. Hello Cat, and Merry Christmas."

Cat stared at him for a moment, the anger leaving her face as she smiled.

"Merry Christmas," she said, the scowl remaining firm on her brow. "Why did you think I was a snogre?"

Father Christmas lowered himself until he was at eye level with her, his smile somehow becoming more warm as he leaned closer.

"It's an old curse that has hung around for far too long. But I believe you might be the key to finally lifting it," he said, offering her a wink before rising to his full height and stepping aside.

"You better come inside. All of you. The evening is approaching and I'm almost ready to leave. If you had come any later I wouldn't have been here."

20

Christmas Eve

William followed Santa inside the huge house. The smell of freshly cooked gingerbread hit his nostrils and singing filled the air.

"I'm not a snogre," Cat said to him as she shuffled closer. "I swear I'm not."

William looked at his friend and thought she looked scared.

"Simon N...Your Grandfather is. He kept Brother Drum hidden for years and even tried to kidnap Flo-Flo. But you're nothing like him. And besides, I meant what I said. You're my friend."

Her worried expression softened.

"He's always been a little grouchy, much like the rest of the fishermen in the village. I only hope I don't turn into one of those furry monsters."

"I'm sure you won't. And like Santa said, you could be the key to lift the curse."

She grabbed his hand and squeezed it. He tried not to blush but felt the heat in his face.

"Are you hungry?" Father Christmas asked as they passed a kitchen door. The smell of baking wafted from beneath the heavy wood.

"Yes," William's father said a little too quickly.

Santa smiled as he pushed open the door and ushered them inside.

"Mrs Clause, we have guests," he said as he gestured for them to sit at a round table that was full of baked goods and sweets.

"I do like guests," Mrs Clause said as she produced a tray from the oven, to bring over to the table.

She was exactly how William imagined her. As round and jolly as her husband with the rosiest cheeks he had ever seen.

William's belly gurgled as he stared down at the freshly baked gingerbread men.

"I was about to decorate these, ready for my husband's trip tonight, but I can bake a fresh batch in a moment. Here, help yourselves," she said as she put the tray down on the table. "Careful now, they'll still be hot."

"My favourite," Santa said as he went to grab one but his wife playfully slapped his hand away.

"You'll have yours later, my dear. You don't want to eat before you fly. You've enough weight for those poor reindeer to pull," Mrs Clause chuckled.

"Reindeer?" William said excitedly.

"Of course. How else would I get the job done?" Santa replied, staring at the gingerbread men longingly. "That and the anchor at Merry Wish."

"And Brother Drum," Lola-Bear added.

"Indeed. It is more complicated when given a little thought. Without all of you, fairies, toys, and Wayfarers, Christmas wouldn't happen. Now, let's take these with us and get prepared."

They left Mrs Clause to her baking and walked along the corridor into the belly of the house. Much like Merry Wish, every wooden beam and exposure had woodland animals carved along them. Decorations and candles were everywhere and a huge Christmas tree stood at the centre of the room, soaking up all the attention. It was decorated with all sorts of colourful baubles and trinkets.

Small flames danced upon candles suspended from the branches and glowing with hues of reds and greens.

"That's the best tree I've ever seen," his Dad admitted, nudging him with his elbow. "It knocks the socks off ours, aye William."

"Yeah," William nodded, then realised that they still hadn't put up a tree this year. Not that it mattered. Not now that he had seen this.

"That's Mrs Clause for you. She's the mother of baking as well as Christmas decorations," Santa said.

"And the rest of the house is beautiful," Cat offered, staring about.

"In a way, it's a lot like Merry Wish," William added.

Santa laughed, his entire belly wobbling.

"That could be because it was built by the same person. Elijah Wayfarer. One of your ancestors. He built this before heading South and finding a strong anchor point on the coast of England.

"Samscritch Bay," William said.

"Yes. Samscritch Bay. Or Christmas Bay, as it was first called."

William slapped his forehead.

"Of course. If you swap the letters around in Samscritch, you get Christmas. But why not simply it call it Christmas Bay?"

Father Christmas pushed his spectacles up the bridge of his nose.

"A spot of bother with the Puritans, back in the day. I believe that was why the letters of the village were scrambled around. To avoid the eyes of Oliver Cromwell. One of the first Snogres to leave these shores."

"Wait, What? Oliver Cromwell was a snogre?" Cat blurted out. "They forgot to mention that in History last year. Wait, is he related to me?"

They left the big room and walked down several corridors, passing friendly elves on the way until they reached the rear of the building.

Santa opened large double doors to reveal a huge stable with dozens of elves running around. When they saw Santa approach they paused briefly before carrying on at a faster speed.

William ran a finger along the empty stable stalls and read the names as he passed.

"Donner, Comet, Blitzen, Dasher," he was saying while Cat read the ones on the other side of them.

"Cupid, Dancer, Prancer, Vixen, Rudolph."

"But where are they?" his father asked as they passed beyond the stables and rounded a corner.

"Here," Santa said as he opened his arms.

William gasped as he stared at the huge sleigh that sat on the snow. It was easily the size and length of two family cars. Made from polished pine it was intricately decorated with gold leaf along the rails and sides. Red velvet seats were carved into the front in two rows while in the back was the largest sack William had ever seen.

"Are the presents for all the children in the world inside that?" Cat asked, raising her eyebrows.

"Every single one of them," Santa replied, gently tapping the bulging red sack. "But don't ask me how the elves manage to cram them in there every year. It makes the mind boggle. I just accept it for what it is."

"Magic," William offered, unable to take his eyes from the sack. He wondered if his presents were in there.

"Indeed," Santa said, and then walking further along he spoke to another elf who was holding a clipboard and was busy ticking things off. "Are we ready, Gooble?"

"Almost, Santa. We're loaded and ready to go. All we need to do now is the final checks and warm the reindeer up."

William wandered closer to the reindeer, gingerly stepping within touching distance. They looked at him as he approached, sniffing the air. They were a lot bigger than how he imagined them.

"It's ok. They won't bite. Go ahead, stroke them if you like," Santa said.

William slowly brushed a hand down the back of the closest. Comet was written in gold lettering along the polished bridle.

He and Cat stroked every one of them and when he came to Rudolph, he laughed.

"What is it?" his father asked.

"Look at his nose, it's actually got a red tint. The songs are true."

"You know," he never used to have. Not until that song came out all those years ago. Then as people started to believe the songs, his nose became like that," Santa explained, shaking his head.

"And does it light up?" Cat asked.

Santa smiled as he tapped his nose.

"We will see. Now, let's get you comfortable. We can't delay. Especially now that we've got passengers to take. With any luck, we can catch some headwinds on the way down."

"You mean we're leaving right away?" William's father asked.

Santa nodded as he reached into the sleigh and retrieved a large red coat. He slipped it on and buckled a wide belt around his belly.

"Extra passengers will slow us down. If we leave now, we can reach Merry Wish within a couple of hours. I can't begin the delivering until then. We need to anchor the sleigh so I don't fly right off the Earth once I reach star speed. All aboard who's coming aboard," he laughed as he motioned for them to climb into the sleigh.

Cat and William climbed up, sliding along the red velvety bench to allow room for his father who was grinning like a child. Lola-Bear and Flo-Flo were next, flying onto the front seat with Santa.

"Can you believe this is happening?" William asked Cat.

"No. I'm expecting to wake up any moment," she said, smiling back at him.

"Wait," came a voice from the stables.

Mrs Clause came into view carrying a bundle under an arm and a basket in the other.

"You always try to sneak off without saying goodbye," she scolded her husband.

"Sorry dearest. You know how excited I get when I'm about to begin the journey.

"I should do, you do it every year. Here," she said passing him the basket. "Don't eat it all at once. You know you always get hungry when you reach the equator."

She then turned to the back seat and passed them a bundle.

It was a thick velvety blanket which matched the colours of the seats.

"It'll get cold so make sure you wrap yourself under this."

"Thank you, and we will," Alfie promised.

They watched as Mrs Clause kissed Santa and then stepped back to stand with the elves.

"Right," Santa said, looking over his shoulder at them. "Are we ready to deliver Christmas?"

They were all nodding, eager to fly.

"Great. Now hold on and sit back in your seats. The take-off can be a little shaky."

He turned to face the front and taking the reins, gave them a flick.

"Go Dasher, go Dancer, go Prancer, go Vixen, go Comet, go Cupid, go Donna, go Blitzen," he shouted and gave another flick of the reins.

Immediately William was thrown back in his seat as the sleigh catapulted forward accelerating faster than he had ever gone before.

The scenery around them rushed past in a blur and then all at once the reindeer galloped skywards, pulling the sleigh after.

"Yeah!" William shouted as he looked down and watched Santa's village disappear.

"Now make yourself comfortable. We're heading due South and should have you home within a couple of hours. I trust young Jack will have the anchor machine ready. Oh, and have the driveway clear for landing."

William's father nodded.

"Bampa will have it all under control, I'm sure," he said. Then turned to William. "I hope."

20

Anchorage

Jack scratched at the stubble on his chin as he stared up at the chimney pots which Simon had repaired.

"Are you sure you mended them properly? It must be done perfectly," he said, his eyes never leaving the stack.

"I've told you already, Jack. The pot is fixed. Ask her, she's inspected it," Simon replied nodding towards Nora-Nu.

"It looks sound," she said, shrugging. "It will have to do. They should be here any time."

Simon eyed the fairy suspiciously.

"They'd better be. And they'd better have my granddaughter with them too," he warned.

It was Jack's turn to snap at him.

"And I've told you already, Simon. Alfie will bring her back. He will bring them all home."

Snow drifted across the drive, the wind lifting a flurry that darted over the fountain where the arctic fox pranced back and forth as if searching for something. It appeared to Jack that the animals were just as anxious as the humans were.

He took his mind away from the chimney. If it wasn't done properly, he couldn't do anything about it now.

"Is everything else ready, Nora-Nu?"

The fairy smiled up at him, her cherub face seeming to light up the night.

"Jill is rounding the toys up now and is placing them around the anchor site. They should be in position soon."

"Good," Jack replied, staring at the open door that led to the anchor machine. He's been keeping a close eye on the snogre and keeping him well away should he try anything. "What else is there to do?" he asked out loud as he went through the lists that were in the journal. "I think that's about it," he answered himself.

Jill then came out of the door with two steaming mugs.

"Coffee?" she asked.

The men took the mugs gratefully, Jack putting his cold fingers around the warm mug.

"The toys are in place," Jill said, pulling her coat tight around her. "It seems like the wind is picking up."

"And so it should. The reason why Merry Wish is here is because of the winds. They're special. There are not many places in the world where the four winds meet. Probably because of the sea, the valleys and the way the warm water goes up the channel. That's why we need the chimney working. It's positioned perfectly in the middle where they all meet. It's the only way we'll know the precise time it'll happen. That's when the anchor must be set. But they'll need to be back before that happens."

"Why?"

"Because of the four winds. North, East, South and West. Like the compass, they'll need each of the points covered by the fairies, including Brother Drum. So you see, they need to be back so Lola-Bear and Flo-Flo can be where they should be."

"I don't like any of this," Simon admitted, his already wrinkly face screwing as he spat on the ground.

Jack snorted.

"You're not supposed to like it. You're a snogre."

"As soon as Cathrin's with me, we'll be going. And good riddance to the lot of you. I'm sick of Christmas already."

"But why?" Jill asked.

Simon opened his mouth to speak but frowned. He went to shape another word yet said nothing.

"That's just the way it is. Snogres hate Christmas. Always have and always will."

He took a sip of his coffee and put his back to them, ending the conversation.

Jack shrugged.

"Are you sure we're not missing something?" Jill asked. Is there anything left in the journal we haven't covered?"

Jack shook his head.

"We've followed it to the letter. I mean, it was written a long time ago and nothing has been added."

Jill stared passed him at the drive. What are the animals doing?"

Jack tuned to find that the arctic fox was still jumping up and down in the snow and the stag was marching up and down, snorting with irritation as he knocked his antlers against the truck. A squirrel was darting around the fountain, running up and down its length and seeming confused.

"They're not happy," Nora-Nu said as she took a step towards them. "Something isn't right. What have we missed."

"Read through that journal again," Simon demanded. "I won't have you bodging things up and my granddaughter not being able to get back."

"I'm telling you. There's nothing in the journal that we've overlooked."

Jill frowned as she stared from one end of the drive to the other.

"Where is the sleigh supposed to land?" she asked.

"In the drive," Jack replied, looking around the snow-covered area. Even the truck was buried beneath a thick white blanket. The stag was still beside it, his antlers working back and forth along the bonnet.

"The truck. It's in the way," Jill burst out. "No wonder it wasn't in the journal. Cars weren't invented back when it was written."

Jack watched as she fumbled in her coat pocket for the keys. While she was searching for them he ambled over to the truck and swiped his arm across the door and then over the windscreen.

"I'll get the gate," he said and walked as fast as he could, his leg protesting with the urgency.

Grasping the bolt he slid it open and heaved the gates wide.

He hated to open them so close to the anchoring point. The protection of Merry Wish would be temporarily broken until the gates were closed again, but with Simon being the only snogre in the village, he doubted there would be any real threat.

Jill climbed into the truck, slamming the door behind her and dislodging more snow from the bonnet and roof.

No wonder they had forgotten about it. It was so buried beneath the snow that it became almost invisible.

Jill began to shake her head and opened the door.

"It's not starting," she shouted.

Jack hobbled back but there was nothing he could do. He was no mechanic.

"Pull the bonnet catch," Simon said as he went to the front of the car. He lifted the bonnet and stared at the engine. "Try again."

Jill turned the key but there was nothing.

"You've got a flat battery. It's the cold. It'll zap all the energy out of them if you don't let the engine charge them up."

"We'll have to push it out," Jack suggested as he rested his cane on the roof, ready to put his body weight against the back.

"You think we can push this truck through the snow?" Simon scoffed. "Two old codgers and a woman?"

"We've got an elf and Nora-Nu too," Jack snapped back.

Simon shook his head as he slammed the bonnet shut. He sarcastically gestured for them to gather at the rear of the truck.

"We've not got a prayer," he said as they all leaned into it, cold hands pressing against colder metal.

Jack strained, gritting his teeth as he held his breath, as did Simon and the elf, but the truck didn't budge.

"Have you taken the handbrake off?" Simon asked.

"Of course I did. I'm not stupid," Jill shot back, obviously annoyed at the jibe about being a woman.

"It's no use," Jack admitted as he rested against the back door, his chest heaving; heavy breaths left his mouth in great white plumes.

"We'll need more men or another truck. It'll not budge otherwise," Simon said, leaning next to him.

"I could give my nephew a ring. He'll be down in the village."

"No," Jack said. "We can't afford to have any more strangers at Merry Wish. It's too risky. There must be another way."

"Sure there is. We only need to wait until the spring to let the snow melt and we'll be able to push it right out of the gates as easy as pie."

Jack glanced at Jill who shrugged.

"I don't think we have a choice," she said.

Simon was grinning as he pulled his phone from his pocket and called his nephew.

"He'll be here shortly," he said. "Now how about you make me another brew? It's getting a touch chilly out here."

Jill seemed as though she was about to protest, but changed her mind. Shaking her head, she stormed across the driveway to the house.

Feeling his irritation for Simon rising, Jack took his cane from the roof of the truck and began to amble back to the gates.

"I'd leave them open if I were you. He's not far," Simon called after him.

Nora-Nu accompanied him to the gate, frowning at the snogre as she passed him.

"I don't like this," she admitted. "I think he's up to something."

"You and me both," Jack said as he pulled one gate closed while the fairy closed the other.

He breathed a sigh of relief as he slid the bold into place. It was soon replaced by a pang of trepidation as an old Landrover made its way up the lane towards them. He could make out two people inside.

"I told you they wouldn't be long," Simon said as he came to join them. He reached for the bolt but Jack slapped his hand away.

"Why are there two of them? And how did they come so quickly? You only spoke to them a few seconds ago."

"I forgot to mention that Penny was with him. They were probably already on the way over. On account of this being where Cat is supposed to be."

"Penny? I thought she was with a sick relative," Jill said as she came to join them. "What shall I tell her?"

Simon shrugged.

"You can start by not locking them out."

Jill grasped the bolt but hesitated. She glanced once at Jack and then pressing her lips together, slid the bolt open.

Simon heaved the one gate wide open while Jack shoved the other one. When the Landrover came across the threshold it stopped.

"Hello Jill," the passenger said.

"Hi Penny," Jill replied, offering her a sad smile. She was about to say something else when she gasped, her hand going to her mouth.

"What is it?" Jack said as he stared passed her at Simon's daughter.

His jaw dropped open as the woman speaking grinned wider as two long tusk-like teeth protruded from her mouth and white fur grew rapidly on her face.

Jill backed away and attempted to close the gates but with the vehicle now in the way that wasn't possible.

"You tricked us," Jack shouted at Simon, raising his cane ready to swipe it at him.

The driver climbed out of the Landrover and stood next to Simon, looming an entire head taller, and as Jack watched, he began to change into a snogre as did Simon.

"Trick, yes. It wasn't hard," Simon said as he stepped closer. "I disconnected your battery last night."

"You had this planned the entire time?" Jack hissed, feeling his temper rising.

"My daughter going away and leaving Cat alone was a ploy that you fell for hook, line and sinker. We had no intention of her going all the way to the North Pole, but it seems, that worked better for us."

"So Cat is in on this too?" Jill asked, astonished.

The snogre that was Penny shook her head.

"Cat doesn't know anything about this. We thought that this year would be the last time Merry With could anchor that fool in his sleigh. Especially as I had made sure that your husband had a little work accident. A little slip of a bolt, a patch of oil on a gangway, fish wire tied between scaffolding poles at ankle height. It was easy. But you chose to return. And with the Wayfarers back we needed to act."

"That was you?" Jill raged and made to go for the snogre, but Jack held her back. "I'm going to make you wish you were never born!"

"Steady, Jill. We can't do anything now. Not until the rest are here. Besides, I've a score to settle with you for the death of my son and his wife."

Penny laughed, but it was Simon who spoke.

"That wasn't our doing, Jack. I'll admit, we had plans, but death was never our intention. Your son and daughter-in-law died in an accident before we did anything."

"That wasn't you?" Jack said, a sudden feeling of loss coming over him. He'd never had proof that snogres were to blame for the deaths, but he had always suspected. If he had known it was simply a tragic accident, then maybe he would have returned to Merry Wish sooner.

"Of course, their deaths were to our advantage," Simon said with a shrug.

"And my father? His body was found at the bottom of the cliffs."

Simon shook his head.

"That was a fight that got out of hand. Both our fathers had a little tussle up on top," Simon explained, nodding back towards the cliff edge outside of the grounds.

"So your father pushed mine over the cliff?"

Simon shook his head.

"They both went over. Both died. Only mine ended up being washed out into the channel. So don't you go getting all high and mighty. You Wayfarers are just as bad. And remember, Jack, it was you Wayfarers that began all this cursing Christmas in the first place. You and those nasty elves."

Jack took a step back, Simon's anger leaching off him as he loomed above, sharp tusks glinting in the snow.

"Now, with your polar bear not here to defend you, you better do as we say."

Jack backed into the driveway, Jill grasping his arm as they tried to put distance between them and the snogres.

"What about the children? Cat, William and my husband – they'll be here any moment and with my truck in the way they will crash," Jill pleaded.

"Don't worry yourself, Wayfarer. We will move the truck, but not before we've sorted you out. We can't very well have you ruining our plans."

Anger flashed through Jack, yet he realised that he couldn't do anything. He had been well and truly tricked.

"Nora-Nu, run!" he shouted, turning to the fairy who was with the elf as they tried to edge around the snogres.

"Run?" Nora-Nu said as she flicked her hand out and a large golden narwhal horn appeared in it, almost taller than herself. "We're not going to run. We're going to see the snogres off."

Simon began to laugh but his eyes focused on Merry Wish and the laughter died on his lips.

Jack spun and saw that all the animals were approaching. The arctic fox with its teeth bared, the Colonel riding on its back, the point of his rifle aimed towards them, the badgers with Teddy riding one and Dolly riding the other, the squirrels and the other woodland creatures and at the head of them was the stag, its head tilted forwards ready to charge.

The snogre that was Penny stepped forward defiantly.

"These creatures cannot fight us," she laughed.

Nora-Nu pointed the golden horn at her and smiled.

"Merry Christmas," she said.

No sooner were the words out of her mouth than a burst of green and red light shot from the horn and hurtled towards the snogre and struck her in the chest.

The snogre hurtled backwards and crashed into a snow drift.

Jack's eyes widened as he looked back at Nora-Nu who turned the horn on Simon and his nephew.

As the second ball of light burst forth, the woodland creatures charged, and all became chaos.

22

The Battle for Christmas Eve

Alfie looked down as they neared the South coast of England. Or what he thought was the South coast of England. With it hidden beneath thick clouds he couldn't see anything.

"How can you tell we're nearly home?" Alfie shouted over the noise of the wind to Father Christmas, fighting the smile that had been making his cheek ache as they flew down from the North Pole. Everything was so surreal.

"Can't you feel it, Alfie Wayfarer? You're a man of the compass, it's in your blood. You can sense where you are, no?" Father Christmas said as he leaned over the seat to look at him with his large blue eyes. "Close your eyes and get a feel for where you are. Trust your senses."

Alfie did as he was told. He closed his eyes and felt for where they were.

A strange feeling came over him. Not vertigo, but something of that ilk. He felt that he was close to home. That it was below them and a little to the East.

"There," he pointed as he opened his eyes to see that he was pointing below at a patch of cloud that looked no different to the rest of them.

Santa laughed.

"See, Alfie – you can do it. Which means, I'm a little off course."

He tugged on the reins and the reindeer swept to the side, pulling the sleigh with them as they began the descent.

Alfie turned to the children who were fast asleep, their heads resting on each other's shoulders, gently rocking from side to side with the motion.

"William, Cat, wake up. We're nearly home."

They blinked as they opened their eyes, and Alfie stifled a laugh as William's cheek burned red as he realised he had been resting his head on Cat's shoulder.

"Mum is not going to believe us," William said as he looked down.

"She's going to see us landing, of course she's going to believe us," Alfie said.

They were all grinning as the sleigh dropped into the cloud, blocking any view from above as well as below. The only thing visible ahead through the gloom was the gentle red light of Rudolph's nose.

"Don't worry yourselves. The reindeer have flown this way for hundreds of years. They could find Merry Wish blindfolded," Santa reassured them, but as they passed below the cloud he pulled hard on the reins sending the sleigh into a harsh climb.

"Something's wrong," Lola-Bear said as Alfie caught a glimpse of Merry Wish and what looked like a battle happening on the drive.

They all braced themselves as the runners of the sleigh struck a hard lump of snow on the driveway before bouncing them back up. Alfie realised that his truck was still parked in the way, a huge hunk of snow-covered metal preventing them from landing.

"Is that Mum and Bampa hitting a snogre?" William asked as he stared open-mouthed.

Alfie tried to take it all in, but there was so much going on that all he caught was glimpses of a blur that his mind found hard to process.

"No, it couldn't have been. Could it?" he said, yet thought he did see Jill and his grandfather striking a snogre down. But then he also thought he saw the elf riding the stag, waving a candy cane over his head.

"I think we better get down there," he said, but Santa shook his head.

"We can't. Not with that truck in the middle of the drive."

"What about the lane? The sleigh will fit along that," he suggested.

"We can't land there either. The grounds are too slippery and I can't risk the reindeer falling over the edge of the cliff. The closest we're going to be able to land is in Christmas Bay itself. But we can't anchor the sleigh from there. And judging by the winds, we haven't much time left to anchor the sleigh."

"We'll move the truck," Lola-Bear said as she climbed onto the edge of the sleigh and dropped off, flying down to the ground and turning into a polar bear as she landed. Flo-Flo had already morphed into a falcon as she swooped down, her beak striking out ahead of her sleek body as she aimed for a large snogre.

"Hurry," Santa shouted after them. "We don't have much time."

Alfie gripped tight to the side of the sleigh as it turned tightly and ascended once again.

"Does this happen every year?" he asked, trying to make sense of the confusion that was happening below.

"No. The anchor only needs to be done once every few decades. The underpinning of the tradition would then keep the Christmas magic strong. But lately it has been waning, I'm afraid this year would have been difficult if not impossible to do. That's why I was so glad you turned up when you did."

"I'm not sure we'll even be able to get it done today," Alfie replied as he watched a snogre swatting at Flo-Flo but was quickly bowled over by Lola-Bear as she crashed into him.

"This?" Santa said, nodding to the fight below "This happens most times I need to stop by. Oh! I see Lola-Bear is making short work of that truck."

Alfie watched as the polar bear put her shoulder into the back of the truck and heaved it forward. His wife quickly jumped into the driver's seat and steered it out of the gates."

"That will do. Now hold on," Santa warned a moment before the sleigh dived.

Alfie felt his belly gurgle as he was flung back in his seat. Instinctively, he put his arms around William and Cat a moment before they hit the ground.

Snow sprayed up on both sides of them as they slid along the drive, the reindeer coming to a sliding halt only inches from the fountain. If Rudolph leaned forward he could touch the stonework with his red nose.

"Are you okay?" Alfie asked the children before climbing out of the sleigh. The fighting around them intensified and he worried for the children. "Quickly, run to the house and shut yourselves in."

"No way," William said. "I'm not missing this."

Alfie tried to stop him but he had already climbed over the side and was scooping snow into his hands. An instant later his snowball was hurtling towards the closest snogre, hitting it square in the face.

"Cat," Alfie began but she had given him an apologetic look before clambering after William to help him make snowballs.

"Alfie, William, your home," Jill said as she came running across the drive and threw her arms around them both. "I was so…"

Her words trailed off as she took in Santa, his sleigh and the reindeer.

"Jill," Alfie said, taking his wife's hand. "Let me introduce you to Father Christmas. Santa, this is my wife, Jill."

Santa smiled down at her.

"Hello, Jill. A real pleasure to meet you," he said taking her hand in both of his. "Now if you'll excuse me, I think I smell mince pies in the kitchen."

"I haven't made any mince pies," she replied, baffled.

"We'll soon see about that," Santa said as he strode past them and into Merry Wish as if there wasn't a desperate battle happening before them.

Jill's mouth only closed as she turned back to Alfie.

"He's amazing. I can't believe I've just spoken to Father Christmas.

Alfie returned the smile.

"Once we've sorted these snogres out, I'll introduce you to the reindeer," he said. "Now, what is going on out here?"

"We were tricked," Jill explained. "Those three are Simon, his nephew and…" her eyes darted to Cat who had stopped throwing snowballs and was regarding her with a strange look.

"Penny. Cat, your mother, uncle and grandfather are snogres. They've been trying to stop Christmas. I'm sorry. They had planned for you to come to the house with William. They wanted one of their own in Merry Wish. But I'm sure they never meant for you to be caught in a trap that sent you to the North Pole."

Cat looked from Jill to the snogres and back again, the snowball in her hand falling to the ground.

"Cat you're not like them," William said, putting an arm around her. "Dad, tell her. She is not a snogre."

"William's right. Santa said so himself," Alfie tried to reassure her. "It's the curse. You can choose not to be a snogre."

Cat looked from the snogres to Alfie and Jill, to William and then back to the snogres.

"I..." she began but one of the snogres cut her off as she came lumbering closer.

"Catharin," Penny said as she morphed back into her human form, an angry scowl narrowing her eyes. She paused feet away from her daughter.

"Catharin Norris-Ogle, you will come here at once. Step away from those Wayfarers – They're trouble."

Cat let go of William's hand and took a cautious step towards her mother, her jaw tightening as if she was fighting back tears.

"Cat, you don't have to do this," William pleaded. "We need your help. You're not one of them."

Alfie's heart went out to her. It must be a huge decision for her to put someone else before her own mother. As he raised his head he found that Lola-Bear was backing away from the two snogres who had both rounded on her, the other animals seeming too small or too injured to carry on the fight.

"Catharin. We can put an end to this stupid tradition. To Christmas itself. It has plagued our family for generations – for hundreds of years. All you need to do is come stand by us. Stand by your family."

Cat took another step towards her mother, and another, her eyes cast down to the ground. Her mother watched on with a wicked grin curling her lips.

"Cat?" William said, but his words were snatched by the wind.

Together, Penny and Cat walked toward the other two snogres, which were now staring at the group of humans and fairies, toothy grins splitting their snogre faces.

They had the upper hand and with only moments left to anchor the sleigh, they had the confidence to know they had already won.

Bampa limped over to Alfie, wincing with each step. He appeared every bit his 87 years.

"We've not opened the sluice gates yet," he admitted. "And I doubt we'll have enough time to do what needs to be done. Where's Father Christmas?

"In the house, eating mince pies," Jill said, shaking her head in disbelief.

Nora-Nu was suddenly by her side, a large golden narwhal horn in her hands. "We've still got time," she said.

Lola-Bear padded towards them, roaring with frustration before changing back into her fairy form. Flo-Flo also swooped down to join them.

"We can still do this," Lola-Bear agreed.

Santa then stepped into the doorway. His pale blue eyes took in Cat and the snogres. He smiled, his cheeks appearing rosier than ever.

"I've opened the sluice. All we need do now is set the machine going and have a Wayfarer standing at its centre," he said, placing the last bit of a mince pie in his mouth and relishing the taste.

Alfie eyed the door that led to the great machine. It wasn't far but the snogres were between them, blocking the only route. And he also knew that the fairies and the toys would need to take up their positions in the machine for it to work.

"William. You will need to be the Wayfarer to stand in the machine. Do you think you can do that, while the rest of us hold the snogres back?"

As he said it he realised the predicament. Three huge snogres, four if Cat was to get involved, against Jill, Bampa and himself. The odds were not good.

Alfie suddenly felt huge hands on his shoulders as Father Christmas gave him an encouraging smile.

"It's a good plan. I'll leave you to it. I might sample some of the gingerbread men that Mrs Clause has baked for me," he said, treating Alfie to a wink before strolling to the sleigh and climbing in, humming 'Jingle Bells' as he made himself comfortable.

"This would be a lot easier if he would help," Alfie said as he pulled his gaze away from Santa.

"He doesn't get involved," Lola-Bear said. "He can't, he's a saint. But we will succeed. You'll see. All you need to do is get my sisters and me through the door to the machine and hold the snogres back."

"Dad, I'm not too sure about this," William said, his eyes making large circles as he watched the snogres gather together, grinning wickedly at them, claws, tusks and horns glistening through the snow.

Alfie's gaze went beyond the drive and through the gate to where he caught movement.

"Me neither. Look, there's more of them," he warned, pointing to the approaching snogres. There were probably twenty more coming through the open gate.

"But it's something we've got to do," he said putting an arm around both his son and his wife. "I've got an idea."

He pulled them in close to talk, only briefly glancing back to find that Cat was standing by her mother, her back to them and watching as the new arrivals swelled their ranks and formed a small army.

23

Lifting A Curse

William waited for the signal, a rush of adrenaline hitting him as his heart began to race. This was it. This was the battle for Christmas. He only hoped his dad had worked things out correctly, otherwise Christmas would end.

His heart sank lower at the thought of Cat being on the opposite side, fighting against them. Standing with the large group of snogres that vastly outnumbered them.

The mission seemed all but impossible.

"Now," his father shouted, holding the sleighbell that was Nora-Nu in his fist. He cocked his arm back and hurtled her towards the group of approaching snogres. Her glittering ball-like form spun through the air until she was above the beasts, then she morphed into a large narwhal.

She fell heavily on top of the snogres, pinning them beneath her. Her body pushed down and smothered all but Cat, who stared on, mouth falling open.

William thrust a fist in the air. The plan had worked. But he soon dropped it as he watched the smaller snogre wriggle free. It was Cat's mother, Penny. She growled at them, then seized hold of Cat and screeched into her face.

"No," William shouted, anger rising as he watched his friend try to back away. He almost went to her but before he took a single step, Cat growled back, her teeth suddenly extending from her mouth as her face became a mask of white fur.

"Cat, no!"

The snogre which was Cat turned to face him, taking on a hungry grin as she flexed her paws, the claws on the ends seeming extremely sharp.

William ground his teeth, anger now boiling within him. He wouldn't let them take her, and he wouldn't let them destroy Christmas.

"Now," his father shouted again, signalling to Flo-Flo.

The fairy's cherub face took on a fierce determination, lips pressing tight and frown growing deep before morphing into the falcon. She flew at the snogres which were Penny and Cat, and circled them, avoiding the heavy arms and teeth as they strove to hit her, their attention away from the elf darting beneath and weaving string around their legs.

"Ready William?" his father asked, gripping him by the shoulders.

William breathed deeply and nodded.

"Good luck," his father said, and then picked him up and threw him onto Lola-Bear's back. "Go."

William held on tight as Lola-Bear lumbered across the drive, her polar bear bounds covering the distance with ease. He glanced over his shoulder to see Penny and Cat give chase. They took a couple of steps before the string the elf weaved through their legs went tight and they both fell over.

"William?" Cat shouted, sounding more hurt than angry.

He couldn't help that now. She had chosen a side.

Shaking the thought from his mind he jumped off Lola-Bear and made it to the garden door. He went through, quickly followed by Lola-Bear in her fairy form, and then Flo-Flo.

Nora-Nu watched them pass through the door before becoming a fairy, the snogres she had pinned beneath, tried reaching for her, yet she was too nimble.

Once she was through the door, William slammed it shut and slid the bolt, feeling a large thump from the other side. He guessed it was one of the snogres. Probably Penny or Cat as they were the closest. But as he looked to the top of the wall, he could see Cat scrambling over, her claws making easy work of the stone.

"Quickly. To the machine," he shouted to the fairies.

They ran across the courtyard and through the narrow passage that led to the machine. The great sphere hung in the air, slowly spinning with the toys in place. Brother Drum was at the South point of the compass marked on the floor, a slow rhythm being played which increased in tempo. Teddy held him steady as the fairies flew to their own compass points, changing once again into their sleighbell forms.

The four winds were picking up and blew down the four chimneys, chiming as they came out of the flues that ran beneath the globe, setting it spinning. Everything was ready. All he needed to do now was to stand over the family crest and the Christmas magic would be released, anchoring Santa's sleigh to Merry Wish so that he could fly at star speed.

He pulled the lever that lifted the sluice gate and river water came running down to set the big sphere turning on the plinth.

William was beginning to think that the plan might actually work.

Then the doorway suddenly filled as Cat came stalking into the circle, looming a good foot taller than himself.

A lump filled William's throat as his heart sank.

"Cat, please," he said holding out his arms. "I know you don't want to do this, not really. You like Christmas. I know you do."

He backed away as she stepped closer, her eyes darting around the machine and back to him.

"I hate Christmas!" she growled, teeth seeming to grow another inch.

"You've never celebrated it. And that's only because your mother hadn't either. Come on, we are friends. You can start to have proper Christmases with us. You'll be welcome every year. Your family too, if they choose to. End the curse. Think about all the children across the world that would miss out."

He held out his hand, opening it palm up.

"Maybe if we both stand in the middle of the machine it'll break the cycle, the war that has been going on since the beginning. Snogres could enjoy Christmas too."

Cat looked at the hand, and then into William's eyes.

"Please Cat. I know you don't want to do this. We're friends remember?"

Cat gave a final grunt that dissolved into a sigh, then slowly tuned back into her normal form.

"Do you really think it will break the snogre curse?" she asked.

William nodded.

"I let my mother throw me over the wall. She wanted me to let her in. That was the plan," Cat said with a shrug.

"I was never going to do it. And I think Santa knew that."

She took William's hand and together they stepped onto the family crest.

Nothing happened at first but then green and red lights began to dance around the sphere, swirling and twisting in rhythmic patterns.

"It's working," William said, then realised that a toy was missing. "No. It's not going to work."

Swallowing his dismay, he gripped tightly to Cat's hand, feeling a desperation rise within him.

The door suddenly crashed open again and everyone else rushed in. The snogres, his parents and Bampa, all scrabbling with each other. Snogres pushed on while the humans desperately held them back. Beneath their stamping feet was the Colonel, darting through the legs to reach his place in the machine.

Time slowed as William watched the small lead soldier leap onto a snogres foot, then jump impossibly high over a paw that came down to grasp him, performing a somersault before landing in his place on the ground.

The moment he did so, Brother Drum picked up the tempo he was beating and the light spread out to engulf them all.

The closest snogre reached out, claw pushing through the light, yet its advance slowed to an abrupt stop, locking it in place.

It was the smaller of the snogres and William recognised it to be Cat's mother, her body now suspended in the air.

A new wave of golden light spread out from the machine, washing over William and Cat, and he was sure he could feel the spirit of Christmas filling him with joy.

Cat felt it too. Her smile spread wide as she reached out beyond the machine and took her mother's paw.

The instant she did, Penny turned back into her human self, the scowl she was wearing dissolving into confusion.

"I, I feel different," she said.

The other snogres slowed their advance as they entered the light and also took on their human forms. Simon stared at each of them seeming as confused as Penny.

"What is it," Simon asked, holding his hand up to his face, the light glowing from his skin.

"That's the spirit of Christmas," Santa said as he stepped into the garden. "And a very Merry one it is too."

"Christmas?" Simon repeated, his grizzled features softening into a smile.

Santa winked at him.

"Merry Christmas. Merry Christmas to you all."

The large group of men that filled the entrance stared at one another, glancing at their human forms in bafflement. Yet that too dissolved as lips twitched into grins and then laughter.

William's parents came to stand either side of him, grasping him in a fierce hug.

"Well done. You did it, William," his father said, a rare twinkle in his eyes. "You saved Christmas."

"He certainly did," Santa said, rosy cheeks beaming with pride. "Now, if you'll excuse me, I've got a job to do this evening. And with the anchor now fixed to the sleigh, there'll be a lot of children awaiting my deliveries."

He treated William to chuckle, hands placed over his belly as he did so. "Perhaps, young William and Cat might want to join me."

William looked from Santa to his mother and father and then back to Santa. Did he hear Father Christmas correctly? Was he really invited to go with him on the sleigh to deliver the presents around the world?"

"Yes please," he and Cat said together. "Can I go?" he then asked his parents.

"Of course," his mother said, wrapping an arm around his father.

Cat then turned to her mother, who was still staring around, a little baffled at the way things were turning out.

"Mum, may I go?" she asked, cringing away from her as if expecting a flat no.

Penny looked from Santa to Simon and then back to her daughter, a smile brightening her face.

"Of course," she said, smothering Cat in a hug and was soon joined by Simon. "And a merry Christmas."

The machine came to a stop although the light still pulsed from its centre and the golden glow spread throughout the room.

The fairies left their places and came to dance around and between the grown-ups, singing 'We Wish You A Merry Christmas."

The men that used to be snogres began to mumble the words, their voices becoming more sure the more words they sang and their feet began to tap in time to the beat Brother Drum was playing.

As Lola-Bear danced past William she took his hand and pulled him after her.

Without thinking he took Cat's and as she followed she grasped her mother's who caught his father's.

Within moments, all the humans, the snogres that were, the fairies and the toys were dancing in the courtyard. Laughter bounced from the tall stone walls as Brother Drum beat a jaunty rhythm.

As William and Cat came near the door they broke away from the dance and gave a final wave before walking through the gate to join Father Christmas.

They held hands as they ran across the snow-covered drive and climbed into the sleigh.

A moment later, the reindeer were galloping across the drive and into the sky, flying high above Christmas Bay.

Father Christmas turned his head to regard them in the back, a smile parting his beard.

"Ready to fly at star speed?"

William and Cat glanced at each other, their grins matching Santa's, a thrill devouring them.

"Then hold on tight," Santa said and flicked the reigns.

24

Christmas Cheer

Alfie stepped out of the dance to catch a breath, Bampa and Jill following him as they leaned against the wall to watch the rest carry on the merry dance about the anchor machine, the colourful light spilling out everywhere and spreading a feeling of joy within everyone.

"I can't believe how much our lives have changed in only a few days," he said, embracing Jill.

"I know. Things can't get much better than this," Jill replied, her smile lightening his heart.

"And little William, delivering presents around the world with Father Christmas," Bampa added. "And the curse of the snogres finally lifting. It's a shame for it to end."

"Wait, what?" Alfie said, a glimmer of trepidation sinking into him. "It has to end?"

"Of course, my boy. Father Christmas will be back in a few hours and will return to the North Pole. Then we've got to hide the toys, the sleighbells, and reset the machine."

"Christmas comes but once a year," Alfie said, the trepidation disappearing as he watched Penny grasp Simon's arm as they danced around each other, laughing as the Colonel rode the arctic fox around their feet. Molly watched on from her perch on the windowsill, green eyes following the merriment and seeming the only one who had no intention of joining in.

"And when it comes it brings good cheer," Lola-Bear said as she took Bampa's hand and pulled him back into the dance.

Alfie watched his grandfather move like a man half his age and couldn't fight the grin that was settling on his face.

Jill leaned into him.

"Merry Christmas," she said.

Alfie placed a kiss on her lips and squeezed her in a tight hug.

"Merry Christmas."

The End

Acknowledgements

Firstly I would like to thank my wife and children for supporting me with my writing endeavour, and for giving me inspiration – especially my three granddaughters, Lola-May, Leonora and Florence Salter. You can guess which characters they were in the book.

And secondly, I would like to thank you, the reader, for giving my Christmas story a chance and allowing my adventures and characters into your imagination.

Printed in Great Britain
by Amazon